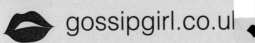 

 gossipgirl.co.uk

Disclaimer: All the real names of places, people, and events have been altered or abbreviated to protect the innocent. Namely, me.

hey people!

Do you ever feel like the luckiest girl alive? Well, you're not, because I am. At this moment, I'm sunning myself on über-social, totally gorgeous Main Beach in East Hampton, watching the preppy boys pull off their pastel Lacoste polos and smear Coppertone all over their sun-dappled shoulders. See, there's a reason any New Yorker who doesn't want to leave the city completely summers in the Hamptons, and it's the same reason people wear Christian Louboutin strappy sandals or fly first class: the best is just better.

Speaking of the best, nobody does it better than Eres. I'm a modest girl, but even I think I look pretty stunning in my mango-colored halter bikini top and matching boy shorts. Okay, maybe I'm not that modest, but why should I be? If you were looking this gorgeous lolling about on a white sand East Hampton beach, you'd be talking about it too. As I learned in my private, all-girls' Upper East Side elementary school, it's not bragging if it's true.

Thank goodness summer is here, and we're finally getting down to the hard work of taking it easy. After a busy June in the city, July has arrived with a gentle breeze off the Sound and standing reservations at all of the Hamptons' best restaurants. Hot and humid Manhattan is close by, but we'd rather stroll around barefoot in our Eres or Missoni tapestry-print bikinis and Calypso batiked sarongs, or steer our platinum-colored Mercedes CLK 500 convertibles up and down Main Street in East Hampton in search of the ever-elusive parking spot and the boys in Billabong board shorts.

We're the boys with sun-kissed hair, driving back from Montauk with our surfboards strapped to our Cherokees' roof racks. We're the girls giggling from our lime- and raspberry-colored beach towels, or partaking in some after-sun pampering at the Aveda Salon in Bridgehampton. We're the princes and princesses of the Upper East Side, and now we rule the beach. If you're one of us, aka the chosen ones, I'll be seeing you around the Island. It seems the season is already in full swing, especially now that some of our favorite faces have decided to grace us with their presences. Namely . . .

the dynamic duo

Just so you know, I can't keep up either. The weather report on these two seems to change daily. Are they friends? Are they enemies? Frenemies? Lovers? You know who I'm talking about: **B** and **S,** and the one thing I know for certain is that they're now certified, official fashion icons. Yes, we've known all along, but it seems the fashion-elite are finally catching up. After meeting **B** and **S** on the film set of *Breakfast at Fred's* last month, a certain monogrammed-velvet-slipper-wearing tastemaker—he of the capped teeth and year-round Palm Beach tan—has decided to keep the two girls at his Georgica Pond manse for inspiration. I hope his menagerie (which I hear includes several lapdogs, a pair of llamas, and two scary-thin saucer-eyed models plucked from Estonian obscurity to star in his upcoming ad campaign) doesn't become too jealous of the new arrivals. Oh, who am I kidding? Those two always manage to make everyone jealous. After all, they have kind of a lot to be jealous of.

summertime, and the living ain't easy . . .

. . . for everyone else. It seems some girls really do have all the luck, and everybody but us is plum out of it. For instance:

would I lie to you
a gossip girl novel

by

Cecily von Ziegesar

BLOOMSBURY

First published in Great Britain in 2008 by Bloomsbury Publishing Plc
36 Soho Square, London, W1D 3QY

Published by arrangement with
Little, Brown & Company, Hachette Book Group USA,
1271 Avenue of the Americas, New York, NY 10020, USA
All rights reserved

First published in America in 2006 by Little, Brown & Company

Produced by Alloy Entertainment,
ALLOYENTERTAINMENT 151 West 26th Street, New York,
NY 10001, USA

A CIP catalogue record of this book is available from the British Library

ISBN 978 0 7475 9696 7

Printed in Great Britain by Clays Ltd, St Ives plc

1 3 5 7 9 10 8 6 4 2

All papers used by Bloomsbury Publishing are natural, recyclable products
made from wood grown in well-managed forests. The manufacturing processes
conform to the environmental regulations of the country of origin

would I lie to you

a gossip girl

novel

Gossip Girl novels by Cecily von Ziegesar:

Truth is beautiful, without doubt; but so are lies.
— Ralph Waldo Emerson

Poor **N**, working every day on the coach's split-level house or sulking by his pool in Georgica Pond all by his lonesome. What's he so upset about? The collapse of his romance with that skanky, gum-snapping townie girl? Believe me, she wouldn't know an Eres bikini if someone threw it at her Clairol nice'n easy #102 bottle-blond head. But hello? I'm available . . .

Poor **V**, trapped in her own circle of hell: living with longtime love **D** but not kissing him, and picking dried booger-globs off her black Carhartt cargos while the hyperactive little boys she's babysitting burp the alphabet.

And poor **D** . . . Well, maybe he doesn't deserve too much pity, since he was cheating on **V** with that flaky yoga girl, and now **V** is stuck in **D**'s little sister **J**'s pale-pink bedroom next door. Besides, he's still got his "work" and a seemingly bottomless canister of Folgers instant coffee. Sometimes it seems he likes bad coffee and bad poetry more than he likes girls. I cannot imagine!

your e-mail

Dear GG,
I don't know where else to turn, so please help me out. I tried to put the moves on my gorgeous upstairs neighbor, but it didn't work out. Then I met her incredible roommate, and it totally worked out . . . or seemed to. We had this romantic summer-in-the-city thing happening and she even said maybe I'd come visit her in the Hamptons. Then the other morning I knocked on her door and she was gone. No furniture, no clothes, no note, no nothing. What gives? Do I call her, or is that just too stalkerish?
— Bummed and Brokenhearted

Dear B&B,
The best of us can be hard to keep hold of. If it's meant to be,

she'll come back and shower you with soft petal kisses. And if not, treasure your memories and chalk it up to the fleeting nature of summer romances. BTW, if you're on the market, maybe I can help heal your broken heart? Send me your picture!
— GG

Q: Dear GG,
All-time weirdest sighting ever: alien imposter version of a couple of girls I sort of know from the city, a hot blonde and a skinny brunette, giggling on the beach near the Maidstone Arms together. They were like Louis Vuitton knockoffs from a street vendor—from far away, they almost seemed like the real deal, but up close . . . Well, some things you just can't fake. Who the — are they?
— Seeing Double (or Quadruple)

A: Dear SDoQ,
Now that a certain blond and brunette pair have become muses to a very famous and flamboyant fashion designer, we're going to be seeing more and more look-alikes. It's going to drive the boys insane. The question is, who will snag the real things?
— GG

sightings

B shopping for new luggage—a quest that took her to Barneys, then Tod's, then Bally. Doesn't that girl ever get tired? Obviously not, and neither does her AmEx Black card, which her mother just gave back to her following **B**'s $30,000 international shopping spree. Yikes! **S** at the newsstand on the corner of Eighty-fourth and Madison, loading up on every available fashion and celebrity glossy, surreptitiously scanning the columns for mention of herself. A girl needs beach reading. A dejected-looking **N**, picking up a lukewarm six-pack of Corona at that seedy liquor store in Hampton Bays. No word on whether he was stocking up for a romantic sunset barbecue on the beach or just drowning his sorrows. Given the shenanigans at the *Breakfast at Fred's* wrap party, probably the latter. **V** and **D** together (but not like you think) at the corner bodega at Ninety-second and Amsterdam, foraging for supplies for their communal home. They're such an old married couple—all toilet-paper shopping, no sex. **K** and **I** at the Union Square Whole Foods, obliviously bumping their shopping baskets into all the other customers while their black town car waited outside. Word to the wise, girls: you might be stocking up on watercress, rice cakes, and unflavored seltzer water to take to the Hamptons, but when you help yourself to five (or six or seven) of the truffle samples, you've blown your bikini-butt diet. Still, those things are good. **C** reemerging from a weeklong hiatus from the social scene. Turns out he's been ensconced in his favorite rooftop suite at the new Boatdeck Hotel on Gansevoort Street . . . and he wasn't alone: a certain brassy blonde whose roots appear to have grown at least half an inch was right by his side. Remember her? I know **N** does.

It's going to be a sultry, bustling July, people, but you know I never rest. You'll always know who's coming, who's going, who's crashing the hottest parties on Gin Lane, Further Lane, and all those tacky Hamptons nightclubs, and who's sneaking around under the cool cover of night. After all, I'm everywhere. Well, everywhere that's anywhere, anyway.

You know you love me.

gossip girl

s and b peek into the fun-house mirror

"Hello? Hello?" Blair Waldorf and Serena van der Woodsen swept into the sparsely decorated foyer of Bailey Winter's East Hampton midcentury-modern retreat. Outside the hydrangeas were blooming, the pollen was flying, and the temperature was rising, but inside it felt cool, clean, and crisp. Blair dropped her salmon-pink leather Tod's carryall onto the zebrawood floor and called out again, "Hellooooo?"

"Anybody home?" Serena pushed her vintage wood-paneled Chanel sunglasses on top of her head. She was used to houses full of antiques, but if she had a summer house, she'd want it to look just like this—sleek, clean, and antiqueless.

"You're here, you're here, you're here!" The couturier to the jet set glided down the polished ebony staircase like an oversize toddler on Christmas morning, clapping his hands delightedly and shouting over the chorus of yelps from the five pugs following in his wake.

Blair swapped three air kisses with the designer and noticed, for the first time, that he was so short his head was exactly level with her chin. After providing the costumes for

Breakfast at Fred's, the teen remake of the Audrey Hepburn classic *Breakfast at Tiffany's* starring none other than Blair's oldest and best friend, Serena, Bailey had invited Blair and Serena to be his muses at his Georgica Pond estate for the summer. They would inspire his new line, Summer/Winter by Bailey Winter, a one-show-only collection of his most exciting summer and winter looks.

"Thank you so much for having us," Blair purred as the five little dogs sniffed enthusiastically at her pale pink South of the Highway–polished toes, clad that day in—of course— white linen Bailey Winter espadrilles.

"Don't be shy!" the designer cried over Blair's right shoulder, startling Serena, who was still standing on the threshold, taking in the scene. "Come here and give me a big kissie-poo immediately!"

Serena followed Blair's example, depositing her hunter green Hermès canvas tote on the well-polished floor and embracing the diminutive designer. The pugs swirled around her, rubbing their fat, drool-dripping jowls against her already-tanned legs.

"Oh my goodness, behave!" Bailey scolded the dogs, though they paid no attention, wagging their tiny blond rumps crazily. "Girls, let me introduce you. These are Azzedine, Coco, Cristóbal, Gianni, and Madame Grès." He nodded to his five bug-eyed dogs. "Kiddies, these are the girls: Blair Waldorf and Serena van der Woodsen, my new muses. Play nice!"

"Should I get the bags?" inquired a deep voice with a vaguely German accent. Blair turned to see a lanky, floppy-haired boy enter the room from the sunlight-flooded hallway that led to the back of the house. Blair could see an almost-black infinity-edge swimming pool through the floor-to-ceiling windows behind him. The boy was wearing a threadbare orange T-shirt that barely covered his caramel-colored biceps, and tattered olive cargo shorts that hung below his knees. Where had she seen him before? In an Abercrombie catalog? In his underwear on a billboard in Times Square?

In her dreams?

"Oh hel-*looooo*, Stefan," Bailey squealed. "The girls will stay in the pool house."

"Certainly." Stefan grinned, grabbing Blair's and Serena's abandoned bags.

"We've got more in the car," Blair informed him, admiring the way his biceps flexed as he negotiated her overstuffed carryall.

"Naughty girl!" Bailey stage-whispered, catching Blair's eye. He placed a well-tanned if slightly orange arm around her shoulders, giving her a squeeze. "He's a treat, isn't he?"

Blair nodded enthusiastically, although the sight of Stefan's taut arms and sun-kissed hair made her think of the one-time/maybe-still love of her life, Nate Archibald. The sun always seemed to work magic on Nate's body. He could be wearing a nerdy polo from back in ninth grade and the dorky pressed Brooks Brothers khaki Bermuda shorts his mom always bought for him, but with a tan he still looked ridiculously hot.

Pulling up to Bailey's concrete-and-glass house a few minutes ago, Blair hadn't been able to help but surreptitiously scan the neighboring driveways for sight of Nate's car. His family always summered in Maine, but she'd heard he was staying at their new Hamptons beach house while he worked for his coach. She'd never been there, but it was around here some-where. Not that she'd really thought about it or anything.

Sure she hasn't.

It was the last summer vacation of her entire life—yes, college would have summer vacations, too, but Blair expected they would be filled with important internships at fashion magazines, archeological digs in the desert of Mumbai, or "anthropological" research in the south of France. In a mere eight weeks she'd pack her new bisque-colored BMW (a graduation present from her globe-trotting and gay but still-sweet dad) and drive to New Haven to begin her life as a Yalie. Until then, she was determined to make the most of her life as a fashion muse. She'd spend her days sipping limoncello and chilled vodka by the pool and her nights kneading Stefan's arm muscles. Or searching for Nate. Or not searching for Nate. Whatever.

"Your house is beautiful."

The sound of Serena's voice snapped Blair out of her reverie, and she stopped admiring Stefan's shapely arms and studied her best friend, who was sitting on the floor sur-rounded by Bailey's dogs, smiling happily. She wore a long white cotton spaghetti-strap Marni dress with purple crochet trim. On anyone else it would have looked horribly hippie Aunt Moonbeam from San Francisco, but of course it looked completely ravishing on Serena.

"I'm glad my humble abode meets Serena van der Woodsen's exacting standards," Bailey replied.

Six bedrooms, seven baths, aviary, pool house, helipad, and tennis court: humble abode, indeed.

Serena cradled Coco in her arms and kissed her adorably

deformed-looking face. The pug wheezed and snorted happily. Serena hadn't rolled around on the floor with a dog since she'd dated Blair's stepbrother, Aaron. His dog, Mookie, had drooled all over Blair's bedroom and scared Kitty Minky, Blair's cat, into peeing everywhere, but Serena had a soft spot for him anyway. She wondered if Bailey would let Coco sleep with her in the guest house at night, like a real-life teddy bear.

"Someone's taken a shine to you, eh, Coco?" Bailey cooed, tickling the dog under her furry chin as though she were a hairy little baby. "Come, come. I'll give you the grand tour."

Blair frowned at the four other dogs, all staring at her expectantly. The last thing she wanted was some mutt drooling all over her linen Calypso tunic.

"This way, girls." Bailey beckoned, leading the five dogs and two girls like a flock of ducks down the cavernous hallway and into the main part of the house. The hall was lined with wall-size Ellsworth Kelly red circle paintings that Blair recognized from a spread on the Winter estate in last summer's *Elle Decor,* and opened onto a massive kitchen with poured concrete counters. A huge teak bowl filled with brilliant yellow lemons sat squarely on one counter. "This is the kitchen," explained their jovial host. "But the only thing you really need to know is that the bar is over there." He pointed to a metal corner table lined with an asymmetrical stack of glass decanters. "Allow me."

Bailey went to work pouring one of the clear liquors over ice and crushed mint leaves and handed two full martini glasses to Blair and Serena, who had to shift Coco under her arm to accept the drink.

"What is this anyway?" Blair raised her dark, perfectly arched eyebrows suspiciously.

"Just a mint tea for my girls!" Bailey emptied his own martini glass in a long gulp, and then poured himself a refill. "And the fridge is stocked, so raid away. Just don't tell me about it—it's swimsuit season, don't you know."

"Right," Blair agreed, inwardly rolling her eyes. Old people were always talking about watching what they ate, but she intended to consume as much Cold Stone Creamery ice cream and Balthazar French bread as she liked and still look glorious in her new ivory-and-sky-blue striped Blumarine bikini.

Yummy.

"Come, come." Bailey flung the doors open onto the sunny bluestone patio. "That's the pool, and that," he continued, pointing at a low, concrete bungalow that was like a miniature version of the main house, "is your home away from home. The pool house. I daresay you'll be quite comfortable there. We've got the A/C cranked, the sheets are imported from Umbria, and Stefan will fetch you anything you need."

Anything?

"There are just two more very important people you girls *must* meet," Bailey gushed, and clapped his hands gaily, spilling what remained of his cocktail. "Svetlana! Ibiza! Front and center, please!"

More dogs?

"Comink, Meester Winter!"

Two leggy amazons burst out of the pool house—their pool house—and rushed toward Blair, Bailey, and Serena. The dogs erupted into an ecstatic barking chorus.

"I Svetlana," announced the girl with ass-length whitish-blond hair and no discernable hips. She was wearing a minuscule neon-orange bikini bottom and two tiny orange triangles over her nonexistent boobs.

"I *am* Ibiza," pronounced the other girl carefully. She had chestnut-colored hair layered to frame her almost foxlike face, brilliant blue eyes, and a bright smile that was slightly marred by two very prominent buckteeth. Her lavender-and-gold striped bathing suit was one of those horrible and complicated cutout one-pieces that looks like a bikini from behind. A carefully placed circular cutout in front revealed her rather fuzzy navel.

Ew!

Ibiza, which sounded more like a brand of car than a name, placed her hands on Blair's arm and air kissed her twice. Blair shuddered with horror, realizing that, except for her excruciating orthodontic issues, this girl looked exactly like her. She wrenched out of the girl's grip and studied the other model, who was, on closer inspection, a diluted version of Serena, minus the grace, poise, and New England breeding. What the hell was going on?

"Ibiza and Svetlana are going to be the faces of the new line, darlings. On the ads, you know," Bailey explained with a satisfied sigh. "You two are the inspiration, obviously."

Obviously.

"They're here to watch you. To *be* you, really," he went on, dramatically raising his martini glass as if he were starring in *Rent* on Broadway. "I want them to capture your very essence!"

Um, hello, creepiness?

"Pleased to meet you." Serena offered her hand to the girls, turning to her own doppelganger first. Serena was always unfailingly polite, but even she couldn't stop shuddering on the inside. Apart from the high-pitched voice and questionable taste in swimwear, Svetlana looked just like her, but not. It was like Halloween in fourth grade when she and Blair had dressed up like their homeroom teachers, complete with wigs, ugly Talbots cardigans, and brown loafers.

"It's going to be like a giant slumber party!" Bailey screamed like a six-year-old girl.

Ibiza and Svetlana giggled fakely. "Pillow fight!" they yelled in unison in their thick eastern bloc accents.

"God, you two are divine!" Bailey threw his glass onto the velvety green lawn and clapped his hands together again in rapid-fire applause.

Blair glared at the quasi–mirror images of her and Serena. To everyone else, they probably looked like happy, carefree, malnourished Barbie dolls, but Blair had always been more perceptive than the average girl. Sure, Ibiza and Svetlana were probably supposed to just sit around waiting for Blair and Serena to rub off on them, but Blair could see something else in their beady foreign eyes. Something calculated and decidedly bitchy.

And it takes one to know one.

These girls weren't interested in being second best. Ibiza and Svetlana definitely had other plans.

Well, then.

Blair turned and grinned at Serena, suddenly very happy that she had her best friend with her. She grabbed Serena's hand. "Let's cool off," she whispered naughtily.

"Good idea." Serena understood immediately. She let Coco wriggle out of her grasp. Then the pair leapt into the tempting blue swimming pool, shoes and all, squealing as they landed in the perfectly body-temperature water.

"Eek!" screeched Bailey as the chlorinated pool water splashed his gleaming white linen trousers. "Now this," he announced to no one in particular, "is inspiring. *Hilfe!* Stefan, quickly: my sketchbook! *Bitte*, dearest!"

Blair dunked her head under the glittering, rippling water, feeling her dark hair swirl around her. She surfaced just in time to see Ibiza turn to Svetlana conspiratorially. And with that, the copycats stepped to the edge of the pool and cannonballed into the deep end, their bones slapping the water.

Welcome to your new family, girls!

n knows a desperate housewife when he sees one

"Nate? Naaa-te? Where *are* you hiding, my little gooseberry?"

That muffled, far-off cry made the fine sun-bleached hairs on the back of Nate Archibald's tanned neck stand straight up. He'd purposely chosen the dingy but deserted attic of Coach Michaels's house for a quick escape from yet another day of indentured servitude in the not-so-fashionable part of Long Island.

Escape, of course, meaning escape to stoned land. Inhale THC, exhale CO_2.

He took a long drag from the freshly rolled joint and blew a plume of warm, dry smoke out the small half-window, straining to hear where the voice was coming from. The voice in question belonged to Patricia, also known as "Babs," Coach Michaels's ever-present and usually sun-bathing-topless-by-the-pool wife. Nate had been working at the Michaelses' Hampton Bays house since graduation—or in his case, semigraduation, since he hadn't yet received his diploma, due to a now-infamous Viagra-stealing incident. And while

Babs had always been friendly—bringing him tall glasses of lemon-infused ice tea as he guided the lawnmower over Coach's beloved lawn, urging him to eat a slice of buttery cinnamon toast when he showed up in the morning, bleary-eyed and ready for work—for the past two days she'd been . . . well, *extra* friendly. He might have been stoned most of the time, but he was with it enough to notice that Babs Michaels *definitely* had a thing for him.

Doesn't everyone?

Nate paused and focused all his energy on listening to the quiet house, but the only noise he heard was the pounding of his stoned, nervous heart. He brought the joint back up to his lips and paused—maybe the pot was making him paranoid, but he thought he heard something. It sounded like footsteps coming closer.

Shit! Nate hastily stubbed the joint out on the rough wooden windowsill, sending a shower of sparks onto the floor. Great—not only was he about to get caught smoking a joint on the job, he was going to burn the fucking house down in the process. He tucked the roach into his pocket—no sense wasting it—and frantically fanned the smoke out the open window.

"Are you up here, Nate?" Babs's voice boomed from the bottom of the attic stairwell. "Do I smell something . . . *illegal?* You know, I was a teenager once, too—not so long ago!"

Nate was still waving his hands frantically when Babs emerged from the top of the stairs. A sly smile spread across her wrinkled, slightly sun-burnished face. Her dyed-red hair was pulled back in a sloppy ponytail. A halo of auburn frizz puffed out around her forehead.

"There you are." Babs sighed. "Didn't you hear me calling for you?"

Nate shook his head, suddenly very concerned about how stoned he was.

"Well," she continued, strolling toward him, past the piles of cardboard boxes and all the old toys and junk that she and the coach had stored up there. "You know what my husband said: while he's out of town, you're *mine.*"

"Y-y-yeah," stammered Nate. Coach was away at some lacrosse conference in Maryland for the week, probably learning new techniques in torturing high school boys. Nate was suddenly panicked he hadn't completely put out the joint. Were his pants going to catch fire?

Yikes.

"The thing is, Nate," Babs went on, idly tracing the handle-bars of a rusted Schwinn bike that was hanging from the ceiling, "I need a hand. Do me a little favor, will you?"

"'Course." he nodded. "That's what I'm here for."

"Well, this particular favor might be outside of your regular job description," she admitted. "But if you'd be so kind as to help me out, maybe I won't mention anything about the fact that my attic smells like a Grateful Dead concert. What do you say?"

What can you say to blackmail?

"I'm . . . I'm sorry," Nate stumbled. "It won't happen again."

Babs laughed. "You can't possibly expect me to believe that." She smiled, pushing past the upside-down bike toward Nate, who was still hunched by the window. "But never mind. I need a hand, and you've got two." She took his now-callused hands in hers, examining them. "Two very capable, strong hands."

Nate wondered if he shouldn't warn Coach that his kids might not look like him for a reason: Babs had probably bagged every grocery boy who'd bagged her groceries!

"What can I do for you?" he asked, trying to sound cheerfully polite, although he heard his voice warble in pure stoned terror.

Babs dropped his hands and undid the top button on her pink cotton shirt. "I decided to get a little surprise for the coach." She undid another button.

"I see," Nate replied evenly. And he did see: some very impressive cleavage, and nary a tan line, thanks to her afternoon regimen of topless sunbathing.

Nice.

"I decided to get a little tattoo." She giggled, undoing the last button on her shirt and letting it slide off her shoulders and onto the floor. "Just a little something for the coach to discover when he gets home."

"Great." He nodded. *Eye contact, eye contact, eye contact.*

"But I've got to take special care of it," she whispered huskily, turning her back to Nate to reveal a tiny tattoo of a butterfly, its green wings spread across the burnished leather of her lower back. "But I just can't seem to reach it," she continued. "My tattoo artist, Matty? He said I have to rub this ointment on it every couple of hours."

Nate studied the tattoo, trying desperately to clear his head. What was he supposed to do in this situation? Babs was okay, but up close her skin looked kind of like a beat-up old baseball glove, and her perfume smelled like the soap in a gas station bathroom.

No wonder Coach Michaels needed that Viagra.

Speaking of him: he'd kick Nate's ass, and not just figuratively, if he knew that his wife had taken her top off in Nate's presence. On the other hand, if he didn't rub Babs with ointment she'd tell Coach Michaels he'd been smoking pot on the job. The coach probably wouldn't give Nate his diploma at the end of the summer, which would mean no more Yale, and basically his whole entire life would be fucked up.

His choices were slightly limited.

"Where's the ointment?" he asked Babs, closing his eyes as he dabbed it on. He searched his stoned brain for something nonsexual to talk about. "Um, after this I gotta get that mower out of the sun, otherwise she might blow. I don't want to start any fires."

Too late, honey. Too late.

twisted minds think alike

"Ouch, shit," muttered Dan Humphrey, burning his tongue on his tap-water-and-Folgers-granules excuse for a cup of coffee.

Ever heard of Starbucks, dude?

Dan stuck a slightly bent Camel in his mouth and tried to simultaneously take a drag from it while blowing to cool his coffee, which was totally impossible. Coffee splashed out of the lumpy, eggplant-colored ceramic mug his mother had - made years ago, before she'd moved to Hungary or the Czech Republic or wherever the hell she lived, and onto the dusty yellow linoleum floor. He was definitely not a morning person.

Dan deposited the sad cup on a semicluttered part of the old Formica kitchen counter and padded over to the beige '70s refrigerator, hoping against hope that he could scrounge up something edible to eat on his way downtown in the subway. He only had twenty minutes to get to his job—a dream gig at the Strand, the tall, sprawling used bookstore in Greenwich Village—and if he didn't eat now, by the time his lunch break rolled around, he'd be half-dead from malnourishment.

Holding his breath to avoid exposure to any unfortunate smells, he wedged his head inside the large, rumbling appliance and surveyed the scene: an ancient CorningWare coffee pot filled with some concoction covered with fuzzy green mold, a white ceramic bowl overflowing with unidentifiable vegetable remains, a clear plastic case containing hard-boiled eggs that his sister, Jenny, had drawn little faces on before she left for Europe more than a month ago. It wasn't pretty.

"Don't bother," muttered a voice behind him. "I looked last night. There's nothing even remotely close to edible in there."

He closed the refrigerator and smiled weakly at Vanessa Abrams, whose status had evolved from best friend to girlfriend to roommate. After many ups and downs—all of which involved Dan's horny, wandering eye—they'd decided they were better off as friends who slept in separate beds, in separate rooms. It just so happened that those rooms were in the same apartment, because Vanessa had been rendered homeless by her newly Czechoslovak-boyfriended totally selfish bitchface of a sister.

"Yeah, this sucks." Dan dropped his cigarette into the sink, where it went out with a hiss. "I'm so hungry."

"Mmmm," Vanessa grunted, microwaving some water in a Pyrex measuring cup, the only clean vessel she could find. She spilled Folgers on the floor while trying to spoon it into the cup. She wasn't much of a morning person either.

A match made in heaven.

She hoisted herself onto the cluttered kitchen counter,

her pale, prickly legs sticking out from a pair of Dan's tattered navy blue boxer shorts. It was bizarre to see her still wearing something of his, something so *intimately* his, when they weren't together anymore. It made him . . . sad.

Every night for the last week, Dan had lain awake in bed, wondering what Vanessa was doing in the next room. He'd hear her get up to go to the bathroom, and think about accidentally bumping into her in the dark, familiar hall of the apartment. They'd fall into each other's arms, furiously kissing all the way back to Dan's bed. He'd rub her shaven head, loving the feel of the familiar soft stubble on his chest, the way her ears were always so hot when she got excited—

Dan suddenly started shaking his head as if his fantasy was water stuck in his ears.

"You okay?" Vanessa asked, eyeing him suspiciously. She shifted from side to side on the countertop, settling beside the microwave.

"Um, yeah," Dan practically yelled, his pinkies now lodged in his ears. "I guess I better hit the road. Gotta get to work. Make the donuts. You know how it is!"

"Why are you screaming?" she asked quietly, her eyebrows knitted in question.

"Oh, sorry." Dan laughed. He downed his coffee in one quick gulp, ignoring the burning sensation in his throat, and reached past Vanessa to grab his folded-up copy of the *New York Review of Books* to read on the subway. "So. 'Bye. Have a good day," he added, resisting the urge to kiss her.

"'Bye," she called after him.

But hello, awkward?!

The rolled-up *Review* tucked safely in his damp armpit, Dan bounded down the musty granite stairs toward the legendarily filthy employee lounge at the Strand. The dark stairwell smelled like moldy books, which should have been nasty but was actually one of Dan's favorite smells.

He had thirty seconds to stash his paper, grab his name tag out of his locker, and report to the floor for duty. None of the bookstore's managers had any sense of humor about things like tardiness. They were crusty, liberal pseudoacademics who resented young summer job kids like Dan, who they all just called "the new kid" or "hey, you," despite the fact that he'd been working there full time for almost a month and wore a name tag everyday, just like they did.

How glamorous.

Dan burst into the tiny lounge, accidentally banging the door against the wall, startling a skinny kid with short, mussed-up blond hair and horn-rimmed glasses too big for his square, wide-eyed face.

"Sorry," Dan muttered, dashing over to his designated locker—a tiny, one-foot-square cubby just inches above the dust-bunny-and-decades-old-cigarette-butt-littered concrete floor. He entered his nerdy combination—8/28/49, the birthday of Goethe, the author of his all-time favorite book, *The Sorrows of Young Werther*—tossed his paper inside, and grabbed his plastic name tag.

"*New York Review of Books*, huh?" asked the blond guy.

"What? Yeah." Dan pinned the cheap red tag to his faded black T-shirt, eyeing the stranger suspiciously. Dan hadn't noticed him around before. Was it his first day? Was it possible that Dan was no longer technically "the new kid"?

"I'm Greg." The stranger smiled. "It's my first day."

Fresh meat in moldy-book land. Sounds like a freaking party.

"Cool. Welcome to hell," Dan barked, secretly thrilled that he now had seniority over someone.

"Actually, I can't believe I'm here," Greg continued eagerly, glancing around the room as if it were the Sistine Chapel instead of a dirty, windowless room in a rat-infested basement. He was wearing a short-sleeved cowboyish button-down shirt and cutoff khaki pants that reminded Dan of Vanessa. The other afternoon when the A/C had blown out in the living room, she'd spontaneously cut the legs off her favorite black cargos to make shorts. God, he missed her.

"I've always wanted to work here, you know?" Greg went on.

"Job's a job," replied Dan, disinterestedly. Of course he knew exactly what Greg was talking about, but he was kind of enjoying mimicking the attitude copped by the rest of the senior Strand employees. It made him feel tough, like he might put out his next cigarette on the back of Greg's hand. "I saw a whole cart of old literary journals upstairs by the elevator. Guess that's what you'll be dealing with till lunchtime."

"Sounds great to me!" gushed Greg. "Am I supposed to just wait down here, though? This guy Clark told me to come down here and that he'd be with me soon, but that was, like, fifteen minutes—"

"Well, Clark knows what he's doing," Dan interrupted. "I've got to get upstairs, but I'm sure I'll see you around, Jeff."

"It's Greg," the guy corrected him. "Did anyone ever tell you that you look exactly like that guy from the Raves, Dan Something?"

Dan froze in midstep. "Humphrey. His name's Dan Humphrey," Dan informed him. "Well, actually my name's Dan Humphrey." Dan's career with downtown rockers the Raves had lasted for exactly one gig at Funktion on the Lower East Side. He couldn't believe anyone remembered that night. He certainly didn't.

An entire bottle of Stoli can do that to you.

"Oh man, are you serious?" Greg crossed the small room and extended his hand. "You're Dan Humphrey? You're *the* Dan Humphrey, the poet? I can't believe I'm meeting you! Of course, it makes total sense—you *would* work at the Strand." He pushed his geeky horn-rims up on his nose. "It's perfect. I can't believe it. I loved your poetry, man. Got any new stuff I can read?"

Dan felt himself blushing. Before his unlikely stint as a rock star, he'd published a poem called "Sluts" in *The New Yorker*. He'd been the buzz of the literary world for exactly five minutes, and though his memories of that time were warm and fuzzy, he couldn't believe there was someone besides his dad who remembered his brush with poetic fame.

"Well, poets have to keep working," Dan lied energetically. "I'm putting together some ideas for a novella. That's why I've been laying kind of low lately."

"Dude, this is such an honor, I almost can't believe it. I'm meeting a *New Yorker* poet. This is incredible."

"It's really not such a big deal." Dan waved his hand like he was batting away the praise.

Mister Modesty.

"This is perfect," Greg continued, shoving his hands in the pockets of his just-below-the-knee cutoffs. "Look, I can't believe I'm going to ask you this, but I've been trying to get a salon going, you know, kind of an informal thing, lots of people who care about books, getting together every so often to just shoot the shit, talk about literature and poetry and films and music. And blogs. But only sometimes. I'm sure you're probably really busy, but maybe you'd like to join up? Or I mean, if you're too busy it's cool, but—"

"A salon," Dan interrupted Greg's rambling. It actually sounded kind of . . . awesome. He'd come to work at the Strand expecting lots of stimulating break-room discussions about the classics and foreign films, but so far the most in-depth conversation he'd participated in had involved two coworkers asking to bum cigarettes. "That sounds cool."

"Oh man, that's great!" Greg cried excitedly, his voice cracking. "I'm still working on all the details, you know, drafting a mission statement, thinking about how to recruit members."

"A mission statement." Dan nodded thoughtfully. "Maybe I could help you out with that."

"Really?" Greg asked. "Fucking fantastic." He pulled a rainbow swirly pen out of his breast pocket and grabbed Dan's hand. "I'll give you my e-mail." He scrawled his address across Dan's palm. "Just send me any random ideas and I'll plug them in. Also, we need a name. I was thinking we could mix up the names of some dead poets, like Wadsworth Whitman or Emerson Thoreau. They wouldn't mind."

No, but they'll be rolling in their graves.

"Cool." Dan pulled his hand out of Greg's grasp and glanced at the address he'd written there. "I'll be in touch," he added, trying not to sound too eager, even though he definitely was. He needed some new friends now that Vanessa was rightfully tired of him.

One word: sad. But also . . . slightly cute. In a seriously sad way.

oh, the places you'll go!

"Okay." Vanessa sighed, kneeling on the fifth-floor playroom carpet of the James-Morgan family's Park Avenue town house. "Let's just do one final bag check and then we are out of here. Ready?"

"Ready!" Nils and Edgar screamed in unison. They were twins and so they did pretty much everything in unison, whether it was spilling cranberry juice on their mother's antique ivory silk–upholstered armchairs or screeching at the top of their lungs (probably to remind their mother that they indeed existed). They were adorable in their own way, but that way was particularly hard to see when you were responsible for wiping their various body parts and making sure they got through the day with those body parts intact and unharmed. And that was exactly the position in which Vanessa found herself. She'd been fired from her first serious Hollywood gig as the cinematographer on *Breakfast at Fred's,* and in a moment of personal and financial desperation, she'd signed on to be a nanny.

Also, she'd been drunk at the time. Obviously.

It was almost too depressing to consider that two weeks

ago she'd been in private rehearsals in a major movie star's suite in the Chelsea Hotel, doing what she loved best, and now she was in a slightly Edwardian attic nursery in Carnegie Hill with a grape jelly stain on her Levi's and two snot-nosed boys somersaulting at her feet, while the movie's stars were sunning themselves on the beach, only a few miles away, in the Hamptons. Not that she was much of a star-fucker, but still.

"Here we go. Tissues?" Vanessa asked.

"Yay!" cried the twins, brandishing two Kleenex bundles. They flung them into the pink-and-green Lilly Pulitzer tote bag.

"Snack bags?"

"Yay!" They whipped in two little plastic baggies filled with cheddar cheese goldfish crackers.

"Juice boxes?"

"Yay!"

"Don't throw them!" Vanessa immediately recalled the pink stains she'd tried so hard to scrub out of the antique chairs.

"Throw what?" Allison Morgan—also known as *Ms.*—strode purposefully up the narrow wooden stairs and into the sun-drenched playroom, her snakeskin Jimmy Choo stiletto slingbacks clacking on the blond parquet.

"Mommy!" The boys abandoned their day-trip bag and threw themselves face-first into the ivory bouclé of her knee-length Chanel pencil skirt.

"Packing up for an outing?" Ms. Morgan asked in an über-fake, high-pitched tone, backing away from the twins.

Very perceptive, Mom.

"Thought we'd head to the Central Park Zoo today," Vanessa explained.

"Oh dear," clucked Allison. "Central Park? You remember what happened last time."

Of course Vanessa remembered: she'd never forget the sight of Dan in neon yellow kneepads and Rollerblades, hand in hand with another girl. A long-haired, spandex-clad, horrifically perky girl. It had been so hilariously bizarre and so completely heartbreaking. Smoking a cigarette, scruffy rock star hair matted, dirty T-shirt, long-to-the-point-of-ridiculous puke-colored cords—*that* was the Dan Humphrey she knew.

And loved?

But of course that's not what Vanessa's militant new boss was referring to. She meant that the twins had ruined their clothes eating Fudgsicles and stayed up half the night yelling, "Fudgie-poo!" because of the sugar.

But Vanessa couldn't stop thinking about Dan. Things were kind of back to normal now. Or almost normal. Maybe it was just from lack of sleep, or the fact that she was so relieved that he'd ditched the blond yoga-toned health-nut bombshell and the old Dan was back, but damn, that morning in the kitchen Vanessa had barely been able to resist kissing him. He just looked so sweet, gulping bad coffee from that lumpy mug, sleep crusties still stuck in his eyes. It almost felt . . . natural, the way she'd always pictured their life together. Except they weren't together. They were just . . . friends. And she probably didn't want to do anything to ruin that, like bury her nose in his warm, delicious, stale-cigarette-smelling hair. No, she absolutely did not.

Liar.

"Listen, Vanessa, I'm glad I caught you." The sound of

Allison's raspy, too-much-chardonnay-last-night voice snapped Vanessa back to earth. "We're heading to our place in Amagansett in a few days. The city's just so unbearably hot, and the boys do so love the beach."

"The beach!" screamed Nils and Edgar, in unison of course, taking the announcement as their cue to race all over the playroom in a frenzy.

"You see how excited they are already," Ms. Morgan observed. "Anyway, what do you say? We've got an extra suite in the top wing of the house—very comfortable, very private. You'd spend days with the boys and be free to go at, say, six-ish, when they sit down to have their dinner. Your pay would remain the same of course."

Vanessa considered the situation: there she was, filling an offensively preppy tote bag with juice and crackers while two little micromaniacs raced around her, yelping about the waves. What did she have to look forward to? Another night staring at the crack in the ceiling of Jenny's room, which still smelled like paintbrush cleaner, wondering what Dan was doing on the other side of the wall, fantasizing about the taste of his warm coffee-and-cigarette-breath kisses?

She hated the sun, didn't even own a bathing suit, and basically despised everything about the beach and the tan, half-naked, thoroughly annoying people who frequented it. But her life sucked just enough right now that it actually sounded . . . not so bad.

"Amagansett," Vanessa pronounced slowly, like it was a disease, or a genital area, or a Far Eastern country she'd never heard of before. "That sounds lovely."

Oh, it is lovely. But only under the right circumstances.

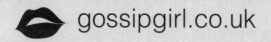 gossipgirl.co.uk

hey people!

I interrupt your regularly scheduled programming to bring you this late-breaking news:

my tipsters are the *best.* You may remember a concerned reader writing in a few days ago about a couple of look-alike impostors who'd infiltrated Hamptons society? Turns out they weren't fooling: the gruesome twosome who bear a disturbing resemblance to **B** and **S** are a couple of Estonian semibeauties who a certain designer has hired to be the faces of his newest venture, a ready-to-wear line he's launching this fall. Looks like it's going to be double (quadruple?) the trouble. And here I thought scientists had only figured out how to clone a sheep! Estonia is so technologically advanced. But the real dirt is on these girls' sordid history. Details are surfacing as we speak! My money's on **B** to freak out first, but before she does, let's all take a second to appreciate the possibilities—couldn't having your own private look-alike come in mighty handy at times? I know I would have loved one this past May at exam time, when all *this* body wanted to do was lounge in Sheep Meadow. And what about avoiding boring family brunches at Le Cirque? Or having an extra pair of hands to do some charity work in our names? And isn't more a little merrier anyway? Then again, more bodies = less space on those overcrowded Hamptons beaches. Maybe ditching those doppelgangers isn't such a bad idea. (Did you really think that getting into college meant I'd forget all my SAT words?)

If you're merely nodding to my overcrowded beaches comment and haven't actually experienced it firsthand, consider this a public service announcement: no matter how many people flock to the Hamptons in the summer, it's the only place to see and be seen. So fold up that laptop, grab a beach bag, and get your booty to the nearest private jet! In a pinch, the Hampton Jitney will do—it should only take an extra couple hours of miserable bumper-to-bumper traffic. But trust me, it will be worth it when you're digging your toes into the shimmering sand. What price glory!

Since you'd all be helpless without me, I'll lay out exactly what you need to bring . . .

packing list for a hasty hamptons departure

— Oversize Chanel sunglasses or old-school aviators. Impostor sunglasses are a little like impostor models: they look fine on first inspection, but close-up they just look bad.

— Clarins SPF 30 with moisturizer. That whole tanned-to-a-crisp thing went out with last year's espadrilles.

— Kiehl's SPF 15 lip balm with berry tint. Just because you're avoiding tan lines doesn't mean your lips should go naked.

— A monogrammed boat bag with matching towel. Sort of the designer equivalent of name tags on your clothes for summer camp. If you lose a towel, keep your fingers crossed that a hottie finds it—and then finds *you* to return it.

— Metromint mint-flavored water. It's cooling for a hot day in the sun. Plus, it freshens your breath, making you all the more kissable. Mwa! Mwa! Mwa!

— Your best friends. You're going to need someone to rub Coppertone on your back, and we all know that summer fling of yours isn't really a long-term solution . . .

your e-mail

Speaking of summer flings, it seems from your e-mails that you all are having some serious relationship woes. Let me help you out:

Dear GG,
I've been living with my ex-boyfriend/friend, and now I'm planning to take off for a while. It's nothing personal—just a vacation. What's the protocol? Do I tell him or just let him figure it out?
—Roommate on the Run

Dear RotR,
Just because you know how your roommate kisses doesn't mean you should go and throw the house rules out the penthouse window. Allow me to share the basics: 1) Food is communal unless otherwise labeled. 2) Give a call if you're not coming home at night—we worry! And 3) If you aren't inviting us on your vacation, the least you can do is leave a note and a gift. (I've been checking out the new Marc by Marc Jacobs beach totes, but maybe that's just me.) Bon voyage!
—GG

Dear GG,
I know my ex-boyfriend is living on the same street as me this summer, but I can't figure out which house is his. Help!
—Stalking the Neighborhood

A: Dear Stalking,
Maybe you should take a clue from Hansel and Gretel and help him find his way to you. If he's like every boy I know, a trail of discarded clothes will do the trick!
—GG

sightings

An infamous lacrosse coach's wife—we'll call her older **B**—coming out of a tattoo parlor in Hampton Bays. I wonder who the experience was more painful for: her, or the tattoo artist who had to see her topless? Former yoga enthusiast **D** chain-smoking cigarettes outside the Strand. Looks like those downward-dog days are over. That is, unless someone else can whip him into shape . . . His little sister **J** all the way in Prague, sketching a totally adorable boy while he sketched the local market scene—nice to see traveling hasn't changed her! A certain monkey-toting Manhattanite, **C**, stocking up on Fake Bake self-tanning cream in Chocolate Mousse. Yummy! Will the Hamptons be accommodating yet another visitor? **V** buying Bermuda shorts and a black-and-white striped boatneck tee in Club Monaco on Broadway. How positively summery of her. **S** and **B** sharing cocktails with their look-alikes—how weird would it be if the four of them became BFFs?!

Okay, darlings, that's it for now. I have a mani-pedi scheduled for this afternoon, and I still can't decide between pale pink Bikini with a Martini, golden-beige Cabana Boy, or bright-coral Shop Till I Drop. Decisions, decisions. At least I can't go wrong!

You know you love me.

gossip girl

b & v break out the birthday suits

"Tell me again," Serena sighed, idly flipping the glossy pages of that month's Japanese *Vogue* as she lay sprawled across the minimalist oak platform bed, "why we're inside on a day like today?"

The day in question was ninety degrees and clear as glass, with the slightest suggestion of an ocean breeze. Serena looked up from the close-up photo of a very blond Japanese model with painted-on eyelashes sucking on an apple-red lollipop. She could see an inviting cool patch of shade under the wide white canvas umbrellas stationed alongside the swimming pool. Today was definitely a lounge-around-half-in-and-half-out-of-the-water sort of day.

"You know the answer to that," snapped Blair, who was angrily riffling through the dark walnut armoire where Annabella, Bailey Winter's housekeeper, had hung all of their garment-bagged clothes. "I swear one of those fucking girls took my fucking Dolce sundress. The one with the grommets. I can't find it anywhere." She started haphazardly ripping dresses off of their wooden hangers and tossing them onto the floor.

Well, that's what maids are for!

"Mmm," Serena murmured. There was nothing special about Blair throwing a tantrum, although Serena kind of hoped she'd pick up the clothes afterwards. But ever since they'd arrived at Bailey Winter's sprawling modernist compound, Blair had thrown more than her fair share—even for her.

Now that's really saying something.

Blair was convinced that the skanky Eurotrash models Ibiza and Svetlana were out to get her. She kept accusing them of swiping her clothes or using her La Mer SPF 45 moisturizer and insisting that Ibiza, the brunette, was mimicking her every move, from her new chin-grazing hairstyle to her wardrobe selections. Serena had to admit the pair bore a troubling resemblance to her and Blair, but they seemed harmless enough. They were just annoying, like the copycat ninth-grade girls back at Constance Billard.

Isn't mimicry the most sincere form of flattery?

"Fuck this," Serena announced, closing the magazine and pushing it off the bed. She yawned. "I'm not going to rot in here all summer long just because we want to avoid some weird girls with buckteeth and cross eyes. I'm going swimming."

"But I can't find my new navy polka-dot Ashley Tyler cover-up," Blair whined. "What's the point of being a muse if I'm not dressed to inspire? If that Ibiza girl *borrowed* it, I swear I'm going to rip her malnourished arms off."

Spoken like a true muse.

"Come on, Blair." Serena slipped a Gauloise from the battered pack on the neatly made bed beside her, lighting it with the silver Dunhill lighter she'd swiped from her brother, Erik. It was engraved with his monogram EvdW. "Just throw something on and let's go. It's too nice outside."

"Throw something on? I have nothing to fucking wear because of those fucking copycats." Blair threw her hands in the air, as though the piles of tissue-thin cotton and fine washed-silk garments all around her were invisible.

"Then just wear something ugly and see if they copy that," Serena offered, exasperated. She loved Blair, she really did, and they'd been best friends for forever, but sometimes she just wanted to slap her perfectly toned little butt cheeks.

"Actually . . ." Blair threw herself onto the bed and snatched Serena's Gauloise from her lips. She inhaled deeply and narrowed her brilliant blue eyes thoughtfully. "That gives me an idea."

"What a glorious day!" Blair flung open the impeccably clear French glass doors to the pool house and strode into the fierce afternoon sunshine, bare arms stretched out above her head. "Come on, Serena. Let's get some sun."

"Coming, coming," Serena giggled, stumbling out of the shaded bungalow, the sun-warmed bluestone burning the soles of her freshly pedicured feet. She held her rolled-up magazine in one hand, a burning cigarette in the other, and her white horn-framed Cutler and Gross sunglasses covered most of her face. Other than that, she was completely, totally, outrageously naked.

"Maybe we should ask Stefan for some iced coffee," suggested Blair, settling her own exposed hindquarters onto a teak chaise. Her only accessories were a tiny gold Me&Ro anklet and oversize black Ray-Bans.

"Vat is going on?" demanded Ibiza, yanking her ninety-pound frame out of the pool. She was so emaciated she looked like one of those send-money-now third-world kids in the TV commercials, totally overdressed in her icky trademark lavender-and-gold striped cutout one-piece.

"What do you mean?" Serena casually tossed her magazine onto the chaise next to Blair.

"Your clothes," accused Svetlana, still in the water, her colorless, overprocessed hair matted flat to her head. "You're not wearing any clothes!"

"Oh dear." Blair sighed dramatically and turned onto her stomach. The sweltering sun felt nice on her bare bottom. "You haven't heard?"

"Heard what?" demanded Ibiza, glaring down at her pert, naked body.

"I guess the latest issue of Estonian *Vogue* or whatever it is you usually read neglected to cover the naked trend." Blair yawned. "It's the very latest thing."

Serena stubbed her cigarette out in a large seashell on a glass side table next to her chaise. She tried to avoid looking at Blair in order to suppress the unstoppable hysterics and probably a snort that would spill out of her if she did.

"Is latest thing to go naked?" Svetlana glanced down at her spindly bikini-thong, which she'd probably mail-ordered from the Victoria's Secret catalog. The water distorted her body's appearance, so that it almost looked like she had actual hips and curves.

Merely an optical illusion.

"Yes, is obvious," scolded Ibiza, pulling down the straps on the top of her cutout suit. Her body, with its circular cutout tan lines, looked like a Twister mat. "Is much better like this. Is European way, really."

"Topless is so *done* though." Serena gave an exaggerated yawn, staring down at her magazine and trying not to lose it. "Blair and I have been going topless at the beach since we were eleven, at least."

"At least," Blair chimed in. Flat on her stomach, she put her head down and closed her eyes.

"Right." Ibiza took the bait. She hopped up on one leg and then the other, tugging off the rest of the hideous suit. It fell to the ground with a wet slap. "Of course, I don't want you to feel uncomfortable, yes?"

"Yes," concurred Svetlana miserably. She slipped out of her sad red polka-dot bikini and dropped it at the pool's edge. Then she leapt into the water and swam away embarrassed, her body a skeletal flash of underfed whiteness.

"Zo glad we can all just relax now, yes?" Ibiza asked, sounding confident but looking uncomfortable just standing there, her Twister-mat body completely naked, like she didn't know what to do with herself. Blair noticed that her boobs were totally asymmetrical, like they'd been glued on wrong. Maybe they had.

"Have you seen hottie that lives next door?" Ibiza started to say in a feeble attempt at casual small talk while naked. She shook her hands out like they were burning up.

"Maybe we *should* ask Stefan for some iced coffee," Serena suggested, ignoring her.

"Yes, sound very good." Ibiza nodded then strode slowly and deliberately to the umbrella-shaded table. She pulled out one of the heavy wooden chairs and curled up on it oh-so-casually. "I call him. Stefan! Stefan!"

Serena held her breath, listening for the sound of approaching footsteps.

"*Now,*" hissed Blair quietly.

On cue, they jumped off of their lounges and took off running, giggling hysterically, over the plush velvety lawn and into the thicket of leafy trees on the perimeter of the large, sunny yard.

"Look, look!" Serena ducked behind the leafy boughs of a baby oak, pointing at the scene they'd just fled: Stefan had appeared, as beckoned, clad in his usual ensemble of tight white tee and cargo shorts. He was also sporting a cute little grosgrain ribbon headband to keep his thick hair out of his brown eyes, which were wide with shock. Ibiza sat before him in all her bizarre pale-and-tanned polka-dottedness. She stuck out her chest, trying to look sexy, but her oddly shaped boobs just pointed in different directions. Svetlana had chosen just that minute to finally emerge from the pool, dripping wet. She picked up her iPod, stuck in her headphones, and began to dance, flapping her pale, spindly arms. She looked like an albino flamingo. "Ratfucker!" she sang loudly, totally misunderstanding the words to the latest Coldplay song.

Serena and Blair laughed so hard they nearly peed themselves. Serena felt flushed and giggly, almost like a little kid again. A very powerful wave of déjà vu washed over her, and she was transported to a moment exactly like this one, only years ago, when they were much younger. She and Blair were changing out of their one-piece Lands' End bathing suits behind some raspberry bushes at her house in Ridgefield, Connecticut. Nate kept threatening to chase them, and they were giggling so hard they kept pricking themselves and sticking their feet into the wrong holes of their terrycloth shorts.

"What the f—?"

Serena couldn't believe her eyes—it was almost as if she'd conjured him. Nate stood in front of them, his eyebrows furrowed, brushing the splinters off the seat of his khaki shorts after jumping the wooden fence between the two properties.

"Natie!" Serena ran over and threw her arms around him, forgetting how completely naked she was. He hugged her back, awkwardly patting her bare shoulder. She giggled and bounded back to Blair's side, obscuring her privates with a leafy branch.

Blair grinned devilishly. It somehow seemed so right to run into Nate like this. There was just something so *obvious* about the three of them together again, even if two-thirds of them weren't wearing any clothes.

"Strip, Nate!" Blair cried, running after him like she was going to pull down his cargo shorts. He ducked behind an oak tree.

"Skinny-dipping?" Nate asked, peeking out from behind the slim tree trunk.

Serena smiled as she studied her old friend or boyfriend or whatever Nate was—she wasn't even sure. That confused expression, those sleepy, stoner green eyes—he hadn't changed a bit. But for once, Nate wasn't looking back at her at all—he was staring, mouth agape, at *Blair*.

"Naked is the new clothed," Blair told him matter of factly. She placed a hand on the fleshy curve of her hip. "Haven't you heard?"

Blair had known he was around here somewhere, of course, but she hadn't expected him to find *her*. Their whole relationship had always been about chasing him and trying to pin him down—she'd kind of wanted to just handcuff him to her bed, and not even in a dirty way, but just so she could keep track of him and make sure he wasn't doing something idiotic. But now he was here and he'd obviously come looking for them. Or, judging by the way he was looking at her, he'd come looking for *her*.

"Totally," Serena confirmed, crossing her arms over her sun-dappled chest. The fact that Nate wasn't looking at her made her feel even more naked. She'd never clamored for Nate's attention, but she'd wanted it. She'd always wanted it. Just then Blair lunged for Serena's elbow, yanking her in the general direction of Bailey Winter's pool.

"Wait, where are you going?" Nate stammered.

Blair held tightly to Serena's hand as they ran. "Get a good look!" she called behind them as they pranced up the flagstone path to the screen door. "And think about us tonight!"

Don't worry, he will.

Announcing Inaugural Meeting, Song of Myself Literary Salon (Manhattan)

Rejoice, righteous wordsmiths! We are pleased to announce a new and exclusive literary group in the grand tradition of the European salons of Gertrude Stein and Edith Sitwell.

We are two humble servants of the written word: one a vaunted young poet and songwriter with a semi-international reputation, the other a reader and thinker who cherishes Wilde and Proust over all else. We are looking for like-minded young men and women who love to read, write, and *talk* about reading and writing, and maybe drink a little Chianti or whatever. Consider the following statements/questions. We'll read every response closely and then send invitations to our inaugural meeting to a carefully handpicked group of discerning New Yorkers.

1. Poetry deserves a more central role in the culture today. There should be an *American Poet Idol* show. Agree or disagree?

2. What is your favorite word? What is your least favorite word? Write a sentence using both at the same time. Example: *Mayhem. Snack. Sitting in the middle of the iridescent-brown cockroach mayhem, Bonita ate a snack of butterfly wings.*

Interested participants should attach a photograph. We need to make sure you're not 12. Or 112.

Looking forward to some inspiring conversation! (BYOB!)

---

n's great escape

"There you are!"

Babs Michaels stood at the cheap Formica counter of her ramshackle kitchen, artfully arranging slices of cantaloupe on a plate of scrambled eggs and buttery toast. Nate rubbed at his bloodshot eyes with the heel of his hand and yawned—for a second the sight of a very tanned woman preparing breakfast gave him a weird flashback to when he was a kid. He used to stumble downstairs to the kitchen of his Upper East Side town house to find Cecille, his parents' Barbadian chef, preparing cinnamon wheat toast or a bowl of Irish oatmeal for him before he headed off to St. Jude's in the morning.

But he wasn't a kid, he didn't have to go to school anymore, and Babs, in her tissue-thin pale purple robe, with her tight, leathery skin, was definitely not Cecille. Besides, he'd already eaten two strawberry frosted Pop-Tarts at his house in Georgica Pond.

"Morning," Nate muttered, watching suspiciously as Babs set the loaded plate on the table, humming throatily.

"You need a big breakfast today, don't you, Nate? All that

sweating and straining in the hot sun." She sidled over to Nate, placing her cool hand on his right bicep, which was peeking out of his navy blue Ben Sherman polo.

"R-r-right." Nate pulled out of her determined grip, taking a seat at the table. He *was* kind of hungry, and the plate of scrambled eggs and lightly browned toast looked sort of tempting, but even in his early morning stupor, Nate could see where this was headed. He'd start eating, Babs would pour him more orange juice she'd just made from the can, ask him to rub more ointment on her tattoo, then suggest that maybe they should take a soak together in the hot tub that Coach never stopped talking about. And before he knew it, she'd handcuff him to her bed and rub the slimy leftover cantaloupe slices over his naked body or something.

The way to a man's heart is said to be through his stomach.

The thought of being naked in bed with Babs made Nate completely nauseated, but he could still feel a certain longing in the pit of his stomach. It definitely wasn't for Babs fluttering around in a purple nylon robe that was barely long enough to cover her half-fit, half-middle-aged-flabby ass, though. It had more to do with the memory of Blair, wearing only the lightest sheen of sweat and lotion, grinning at him naughtily when he discovered her the day before in his extremely gay neighbor's yard. He'd seen her naked lots of times, but standing there in the broad daylight, her delicate shoulders a little browner than the rest of her, she'd never looked more beautiful. He'd spotted the tiny familiar apple-shaped birthmark on her hip and had had to will himself not to grab her and kiss it.

"What's the matter, hon?" Babs wondered, stepping behind

his chair and leaning over him so that her weirdly hard boobs were sort of rubbing against his upper back. "You're not hungry this morning?"

Bursting out of his chair as if he'd been electrocuted, Nate's voice came out much more loudly than he'd planned: "You know, I should, um, well, I need to make a telephone call."

"A phone call?"

"Yeah." He blushed deeply. "Is that okay? I mean, can I have your permission? I know I'm technically on the job and all."

"You don't need *my* permission," she whispered. "There's nothing I would ever forbid you to do, Nate. *Nothing.*"

"Thanks!" He practically sprinted out of the kitchen and onto the back deck. Fumbling in the deep pocket of his cargo shorts for his Motorola Pebl, he started scrolling through his address book and quickly dialed the first entry: Anthony Avuldsen, his lacrosse teammate and the guy who'd already saved him once that summer, when he'd found himself entangled in a complicated romance with a hot townie chick who'd turned out to be more trouble than she was worth.

Don't they all?

Nate was on the verge of hanging up after five rings, when Anthony answered with a friendly, exaggerated shout. "Whassup?"

"Dude. Where are you?"

"On my way to the beach," Anthony yelled over the car stereo, blasting AC/DC's "Back in Black" so loud that his phone shook. "Can you hang out?"

Nate stared out at the small, shimmering, rectangular-shaped pool and the slightly overgrown lawn beyond it. The idea of mowing that grass made him want to cry; the thought of turning around and going back into that house and getting molested by Babs made him want to hurl.

Talk about a rock and a hard place.

"Hang out," Nate repeated slowly. "Yeah, let's do that. I'm at Coach's place in the Bays. Pick me up?"

"Pick you up?" screamed Anthony. "Cool, yeah, whatever. Give me ten minutes."

Nate shoved the phone back into his pocket and inhaled deeply, steeling his nerves.

"Everything okay?" Babs opened the sliding glass porch door and trotted outside. Her purple robe had come undone and was hanging off her shoulders like a cape, revealing her complicated, lacy, animal-print underthings. They reminded Nate of the kind of bathing suit his eccentric French now-dead grandmother had worn during a family trip to the Turks and Caicos when he was a kid.

Oh, how alluring!

"I'm actually not feeling that well." He wasn't even lying, really, since the thought of what might happen if he didn't get out of there made him feel totally queasy. Wincing in pain—but trying not to overdo it—Nate let out a pathetic cough.

"Poor boy," she cooed, using one hand to cinch her flimsy robe closed. She placed her other palm against his furrowed brow. "You do feel a little warm."

Maternal instinct and *Basic Instinct*—what a disturbing mix.

"Yeah," he agreed, backing away. "I don't know if I can tackle the lawn today."

"No, of course not. We should get you out of those clothes and right into bed. I can make you some nice herbal—"

"I should really just go," Nate interrupted the disturbing

quasi-porno scenario Babs was describing. He didn't want to trade her Mrs. Robinson fantasies for some skanky nurse setup. "In fact, I think I hear my ride outside."

"You just rest and take it easy," Babs cooed. "Don't you worry about work. I'll tell Coach you need a rest. He's wearing you down."

"Thanks, Mrs. M." Nate nodded gratefully as he bounded off the porch. Forgetting that he was supposed to be sick, he whooped with delight when he heard a car horn and saw Anthony's black BMW turn recklessly into the coach's driveway. *Saved.*

"You sure you're just playing sick?" Anthony momentarily took his eyes off the road to study Nate, who was sunk low in the cream-colored reclined leather seat, shielding his eyes from the bright sunlight with his hand.

"No, dude, I'm fine," Nate assured him, fiddling with the dashboard vents so that the cool blast of A/C was aimed directly at his face. "Babs was just, you know, coming on kind of strong."

"No shit!" Anthony laughed, turning down the stereo, which was blaring the latest Reigning Sound album. "This I have to fucking hear."

"Nothing to hear," Nate mumbled, grinning despite himself. "Believe me, it'll give you nightmares for fucking weeks."

Nate stared out the window at the landscape whizzing by: the fields of green grass, the rich blue sky, the weather-beaten, enormous shingled houses, all of it blurred together, a rush of images he couldn't separate into their various parts, almost the same way that the summer had been nothing but a stream of various moments he couldn't separate into distinct events. He sighed. There was just something incredibly depressing about realizing that the only memorable moments of the summer had been a total bust of a party in the city where he'd been abandoned by his date, and yesterday, when he'd caught Blair and Serena skinny-dipping or whatever the hell they were doing.

"I saw Blair Waldorf and Serena van der Woodsen naked yesterday," Nate announced suddenly, reaching for the joint he had prerolled and stashed in somebody's leftover pack of Marlboros that morning. He rolled down the window and lit it up.

"Threesome?" Anthony asked, nodding at Nate to hand him one of the cigarettes. "You are one lucky fucker."

Nate shook one loose and passed it to his left. "Nah," he explained, though a very intriguing mental picture was starting to take shape in his head.

Oh, really?

"They were, like, skinny-dipping in my neighbor's yard," he continued, exhaling a cloud of pot smoke out the window. "It was so weird."

"Skinny-dipping?" repeated Anthony, deftly lighting his cigarette and making a left turn at the same time. "No shit."

"Blair, man, she's just . . ." Nate trailed off as the image of Blair, naked, a little sweaty, laughing at him, clouded his vision. He just wanted to hold her again.

"I hear you, dude," Anthony agreed, nodding vigorously. "I mean, you've got, like, a *thing*. And it's our *last summer*. It's like . . . fucking carpe fucking diem, right?"

"Carpe diem . . ." Nate pondered this. Seize the day. He took another deep drag and swallowed, closing his eyes.

Carpe fucking diem. What an idea. It was downright . . . inspiring. He turned and smiled appreciatively at Anthony. He was a genius.

Or maybe he was just high?

"Seriously, man," Anthony continued, holding the roach. "I've been telling you, haven't I? It's time to get serious about having a good time."

Nate nodded. It *was* time for him to get serious about having a good time. Fuck Coach Michaels and his horny wife, fuck the lawn, and fuck responsibility. He was going to seize the fucking day.

And maybe someone else, too.

the lost art of letter writing

FROM: Steve N. <<u>holdencaulfield1@yodel.com</u>>
TO: <<u>anon-239894344329894344@craigslist.org</u>>
Subject: Re: Announcing Inaugural Meeting,
Song of Myself (Manhattan)
Date: 9 July, 16:37:07

To whom it may concern:

It was with great delight that I read your
announcement. I desperately want to be
surrounded by like-minded peers who are as
passionately devoted to the power of the
written word as I am.

In the spirit of true iconoclasm, I
decline to answer any of your questions.
I suspect that you're only really interested
in independent spirits who aren't willing
to submit to your silly queries. Rest
assured, I live by the book and I shall
die by the book.

Regards,
Steve

FROM: Cassady Byrd <brontebyrd@books.com>
TO: <anon-239894344329894361@craigslist.org>
Subject: Re: Announcing Inaugural Meeting,
Song of Myself (Manhattan)
Date: 9 July, 20:04:39

I couldn't believe it when I saw your
posting. Right on, motherfuckers! I'm
really looking forward to getting together
and talking . . . maybe more!!!!

My fave verb is "to love." My least fav
verb is "to hate." You're gonna hate how
much you love me. Burp!

My pic is attached...

xoxo
CB (aka Charlotte Brontë)

FROM: Bosie <lord_alfred_douglas@earthlink.com>
TO: <anon-239894344329895002@craigslist.org>
Subject: Re: Announcing Inaugural Meeting,
Song of Myself (Manhattan)
Date: 9 July, 22:31:14

Saw your ad. Violently intrigued.

My favorite books:
The Picture of Dorian Gray, Oscar Wilde
Interview with the Vampire, Anne Rice

Favorite movie: Party Monster starring
Macaulay Culkin

Favorite song: "Walk on the Wild Side" by
Lou Reed

Favorite word: Bite
Least favorite word: Choke
I bit him and choked.

As you can see from my pic, I'm a guy who
likes to dress up.

when it comes to the hamptons, v's a total virgin

"Here we are!" announced Ms. Morgan as she navigated her cream-colored Mercedes into a circular pale-pink crushed-seashell driveway.

Finally. After a grueling four hours stuck in traffic on the Long Island Expressway, they had finally arrived at the James-Morgan-Grossmans' gray-shingled nouveau-Victorian Amagansett mansion. Vanessa stepped anxiously out of the car, feeling the foreign crunch of the seashells under her feet. The sky overhead was turning a dusky sunset pink, and the air smelled like a far-off barbecue and freshly mown grass. She felt a sudden wave of relief—maybe getting out of the city really was just what she needed.

Ms. Morgan stepped ahead of her, pushing the heavy antique-red front door open. The boys scrambled inside, jostling Vanessa, who was smiling goofily at nothing in particular. Not that Vanessa cared about these things, or usually even noticed, but she couldn't help but gape at, well, all of it. The double-height windows framing the front entryway. The preppy blue-and-white nautical-striped bins filled with beach supplies just inside the front door. The massive living room spilling out in front of her. The inviting turquoise pool just beyond it. It was all so unlike her—but then again, everything that was like her had totally sucked lately. Maybe she should embrace the easy, sunny life that was right here, right in front of her? Maybe all that dark thinking wasn't helping anything?

Vanessa followed the boys into the massive kitchen, where Ms. Morgan was checking the notes the maid, gardener, and pool boy had left behind. Everything was so . . . taken care of. Vanessa could just see the hot summer days ahead of her: Reading *The New Yorker* poolside, occasionally stopping to photograph its glistening surface in black and white. She'd trot inside and fix herself a smoked gouda sandwich from the stocked kitchen, then eat it while wandering the perimeter of the well-manicured property, enjoying the peace and quiet.

Home, sweet home.

"*Mommmmmmeeeeee, we're hunnnngggggrrrrrrrrrrrrrrrrrry,*" Edgar whined, snapping Vanessa out of her reverie. Oh right, *them*.

"Vanessa will fix you something." Ms. Morgan smiled and patted his head, without bothering to glance at her.

"Right. Sure." Vanessa set down her black army-navy duffel bag on the polished blond-wood floor and opened the heavy stainless-steel fridge. Inside were piles of fresh produce, containers of orzo salad, and curried salmon filets garnished with yellow currants. Where were the cold leftover chicken nuggets, or at least the PB and J?

Behind her, Edgar and Nils began a wrestling match in the middle of the floor. Vanessa usually let them do this, hoping they would tire themselves out like the puppies she'd once filmed at the Union Square dog run. She'd been hoping to catch a dogfight or see one of those rat-eating hawks the city had released swoop down to pick up a Chihuahua, but had been forced to settle for puggle playtime instead. She figured that eventually the boys would flop onto their backs like the dogs, their tongues hanging out to the side, panting.

"Boys!" Ms. Morgan barked, and then smoothed her knife-pleated khakis. Her ivory tank top was trimmed with a thick brown satin sash. Looking at her weirdly taut face and defined cheekbones, it was hard to tell if she was thirty-two or fifty-five. "You can head upstairs to get ready for dinner."

She turned back to Vanessa, the wooden heels of her huarache sandal wedges clacking on the floor. "Vanessa, we'll be having the salmon filets, and if you could just throw together a little fresh salad, maybe a dill-yogurt sauce for the fish? That would be lovely."

Wait. Throw together? What did Vanessa look like, the . . . the . . .

Help? Oh. Right. Except she'd never cooked anything but boiled ziti with jarred Ragu in her life.

"You got it," Vanessa told her as she started searching for dill in the produce drawer. Upstairs she could hear the boys making explosion noises and then screaming. She turned around to hold up a pile of leafy herbs—was this dill? coriander? crab-fucking-grass?—when she was met with a frightening sight.

Ms. Morgan's pale, skinny, dimpled ass. Oh. My. God. Vanessa quickly swiveled around again. Even with the refrigerated air hitting her in the face, she could feel her cheeks burning. Loudly clearing her throat—had Ms. Morgan just forgotten she was there or what?—she turned back, holding the herbs directly in front of her face.

She peeked out from behind the greens only to see her employer, arms akimbo, standing in only her wooden huarache sandals, a sheer apple-red thong, and a lacy black bra.

"Something wrong?" she asked.

"Um, no, of course not." Vanessa began a sudden, uncharacteristic cuticle examination. Her hands sure were rough! But she couldn't help sneaking a sidelong glance as Ms. Morgan, liberated woman of the twenty-first century, tugged off her bra and let it fall, oh-so-casually, onto the arm of a kitchen chair.

Vanessa willed herself to look her boss in the face. "Um, could you excuse me for a second? I'd like to put my things in my room." She *had* to get out of there.

"Top of the third staircase." Ms. Morgan started rooting around in her monogrammed canvas boat bag, presumably for something to wear.

Let's hope so!

Vanessa threw her army-navy-store duffel over her shoulder and took the wide wooden staircase two steps at a time. She tried to shake the image of Ms. Morgan's thong from her mind. Who even wore thongs, besides overeager thirteen-year-olds who liked them peeking out above their low-rise jeans?

Très passé.

And whatever happened to boundaries? It was as if Vanessa were the family cat, not an actual human being. She needed to be back in the real world, among people who respected her and didn't just act like she was a piece of furniture. She'd been in the picture-perfect Hamptons for no more than fifteen minutes, and she was already ready to leave.

Arriving at the third set of stairs, Vanessa climbed toward her attic suite. At least she'd have some privacy and maybe even a little luxury up here, right? She reached the top step, and glanced around, looking for a door she could shut. But no, the stairs went straight into the attic-room, where the pitched ceiling was so low, she had to duck to step inside. What. The. Fuck.

Taking heaving, pseudocalming breaths, she walked straight down the middle of the hot, stuffy room—the only possible route she could take without ducking. She dropped her bag on the floor and tried to push the one small window open. Stuck. More than stuck. *Painted shut.* Shit, shit, shit.

Vanessa stripped off her suddenly sweaty faded black T-shirt and unzipped her duffel. She pushed aside her hair trimmers and the yellow-and-black bumble-bee-striped one-piece bathing suit that she'd swiped from Jenny's underwear drawer, looking for her black ribbed cotton tank top.

"Great, you found it."

She turned to see Ms. Morgan, now thankfully wearing a white sundress, standing at the top of the attic stairs. Good, she was dressed. Vanessa, unfortunately, was not.

This wasn't quite the hot summer she'd had in mind.

Air Mail - Par Avion - July 10

Hey Dan!

How's everything going in the city? I looooove Prague. I've been spending my afternoons at little outdoor cafés, pretending to sketch but really checking out all the European boys—I mean sights! (There's no harm in looking, right?) So really the only thing I miss is you and Dad. Please write back. Don't worry, you don't have to send a novel, just a few lines. Knowing you, you'll probably send a haiku.

Love you!

Jenny

reading is fundamental

Taking the rickety Strand steps two at a time, Dan made it from the main floor to the basement-level employee lounge in about thirty seconds, by far a personal best. He'd been pretty down ever since last night, when he'd come home from reading the salon member e-mails with Greg to find a yellow Post-it note on the refrigerator addressed to both him and Rufus. It was written in Vanessa's weirdly boyish handwriting: *Off to the Hamptons for work. Will e-mail with details. Left half a turkey sandwich in fridge. –V.* Dan had opened up the fridge to find the sandwich with another Post-it stuck to it. It said simply: *Eat me.* He couldn't believe she was just . . . gone.

He'd thrown himself into work all day, trying to keep his mind off of her, which had suddenly completely paid off while he was shelving outdated biographies. The empty feeling inside of him had instantly filled with excitement. And he *had* to share.

Dan shoved the door marked PRIVATE open with his shoulder, crying out at the top of his lungs, "Greg? You in here?"

Of course it was totally unnecessary to shout, since the room was about the size of an elevator. Greg was inside, digging in his cruddy locker.

"What's up?" Greg looked a little startled but smiled broadly, pushing his tortoiseshell frames back up his long, slender nose. He slammed the vomit-green locker door shut. "What's going on? I'm just knocking off for the day."

"You're never going to believe what I found." Dan brandished a tiny, tattered chocolate brown hardback. "The second I saw it, I grabbed it off the shelf and ran down here." Technically, employees weren't supposed to leave the floor when they were on a shift—there wasn't even an only-in-an-emergency clause—but Dan had always lived by the rule that rules were made to be broken.

"What is it?" Greg asked excitedly, stepping over the low, wooden bench that was screwed to the floor.

"Ta-da!" Dan waved the book in the air above his head. "Just guess, first. Take a guess, please."

"I can't!" Greg reached out playfully and tried to grab the book from him.

"No you don't." Dan tucked the volume behind his back.

Greg reached around him, still trying for the book. "Let me see, come on."

Dan brought the book in front of him, holding it faceup on his palms. "I hold in my hand an out-of-print masterpiece . . . by one of the most important midcentury American novelists . . . published by a seminal San Francisco publishing house . . . in 1952 . . ."

"Shut." Greg sat down on the bench, as though he might faint. "Up."

"I'm serious," Dan confirmed. "*The Poet's Wake!* By Sherman fucking Anderson fucking Hartman."

"That's, like, the Holy Grail or something," Greg muttered in awe. "Can I see it?" he asked, his voice wavering.

"Just be careful. Some of the pages are pretty moth-eaten, which is really tragic, but I guess we can't complain, I mean, given how hard it is to find a copy of this anywhere. I've heard stories about people unearthing them in old used bookshops in Midwest college towns, but right here in New York City? What are the odds?"

Greg placed his hands over Dan's, enveloping both Dan's fingers and the book within his grasp.

Hey, grabby.

"I've got a better idea actually, Dan," Greg whispered seriously, knitting together his fine, blond eyebrows. "Why don't you read me a passage?"

Dan shrugged. He *did* have a pretty good reading voice. He glanced at his watch. He was supposed to be upstairs, shelving books, but no one ever came into the employee lounge—he could afford to spend a few minutes. Besides, some things were just more important than work.

Clearing his throat, Dan flipped through the book to a random point and then began reading:

"*Emily arrived some time after midnight. She'd taken the train. She looked the way he had always pictured her, in his late-night fever dreams, when he'd thrown down his pen and pushed his paper off of his desk, unable to write, unable to concentrate, unable to think about anything other than her graceful neck, the curve of her hip. She looked like the very idea of a woman, and wasn't that better, he wondered, than the reality*" *of the situation? Weren't ideas, when all is said and done, so superior to reality?"*

Dan stood in silence, still cradling the tattered volume reverentially, and Greg just sat there, staring up at Dan the way you'd stare up at a complicated stained-glass window, or at someone undressing in front of an apartment window, high above.

"It's a crime," Dan muttered darkly. "How could this be out of print?"

"It is a crime," Greg agreed, standing and placing his hands on top of the book. Dan looked at his wide-open brilliant green eyes behind the lenses of his chunky glasses. "Thank goodness there are people like us to keep things like this alive."

"You're right." Dan nodded solemnly.

"Dan," Greg whispered huskily, "I'm really glad we met."

"Me too," Dan agreed, checking his watch again—he didn't want to be away from work for too long, but before he could even figure out what the numbers on the face of his Casio calculator-watch were telling him, he felt Greg's long arms wrap around him.

"This is such a good omen for our first meeting tomorrow." Greg's hot breath tickled Dan's neck as he hugged him. "We'll have so much to talk about."

"Y-y-y-yeah," Dan stammered. Wow, Greg was sort of a geek, but he really did genuinely appreciate how cool the book was. "Here, why don't you hold on to this for me?" he offered, handing Greg the book.

Greg hugged him again, even harder this time. "Wow," he gasped. "I'm overwhelmed."

Dan grinned at him and headed upstairs. Why did he always attract the geeks?

Um, maybe because he was kind of a geek himself?

hey people!

Just when you thought it couldn't get any hotter, the thermometer rises another ten degrees. Or maybe that's just my computer—it's practically overheating from your steamy e-mails! It seems people are responding to the temperature by shedding clothes and getting wet . . . and giving the whole neighborhood a show.

What in tarnation am I talking about now? Well, we all know that in the Hamptons, you can't throw a stone without hitting someone you know (like it's any different in Manhattan?!) Here, though, we have actual *yards* and *fences.* Crazy concept, huh? Rows upon rows of hedges separating the fabulous and beautiful from the fabulous and beautiful. They say good fences make good neighbors, so we should all stay strictly within our own property, I suppose. But what if your neighbor is hot and occasionally naked? This is all a hypothetical, of course . . . I don't actually know of anyone who skinny-dips in their pool and then invites the neighbors for a visit. But I've been hearing rumors about **B** and **S** doing just that, and you know those girls are always setting trends. You heard it here first: time for that fence to come down, people. Screw fences. Good neighbors make good fun.

So hello neighbor boys, come and find me. I'm lying out by my pool, enjoying my own form of A/C: alcohol/college boys. Yawn. Just another day at the office.

Dear GG,

I know I should be out there at the beach with the rest of civilized society, but I'm unfortunately trapped in the city for summer school. Who knew they were really so serious about that whole attendance policy thing? Anyway, I'm freaking dying over here, it's so hot. Help!
—Sweltering in the City

 Dear SITC,

Poor thing. Sounds like you could use your own doppelganger right now! But if that's not an option, here are some quick fixes to stay cool in the city:

1) Find your nearest rooftop pool. If you don't have a friend with her own (or if she's out of town too), try Soho House or the Hotel Gansevoort. If you're really desperate, buy yourself a kiddie pool, bring it up to your roof, and don't forget the hundred bottles of Evian. Now that's what I call a private party.

2) The A/C at Barneys is to die for. I suppose it isn't terribly sunny, but if you're trying on bikinis, it's *almost* like being at the beach.

3) Three words: Tasti D-Lite. (Or is that a two-word hyphenate?) Okay, so Tasti D is totally five years ago, but you know you want something cool and sweet. And if you're really not going to make it to the beach this summer, do me the favor of forgetting about the calories and slurping up some hazelnut gelato from Cones. Yum.

4) You did say you were in summer school, right? Um, hello, isn't it air-conditioned? If you don't know the answer, you better check the attendance policy again!

—GG

beach blanket bingo rules and regulations

For you lucky ones staying cool at the beach, don't worry, I haven't forgotten about you either. The most important thing to remember this summer—and this is for your own good, as well as everyone else's—is that when New Yorkers transport their social scene from the chic Manhattan bars to the sandy Hamptons beaches, we transport our social rules as well. After all, we have to have *some* kind of order in place. So for those not in the know, the unspoken rules of beach etiquette that you absolutely must obey are:

1) Wear big sunglasses if you're going to stare. And you know you're going to.

2) Leave at least four feet between your towel and that of your neighbor (and that is the bare minimum, only in the direst of situations.) If you think being packed like sardines in a hot subway car is bad, imagine feeling that way for four hours straight with hardly any clothes on. Nobody needs to be that up close and personal.

3) I don't care if you're Ricky Martin—no Speedos, please! Actually, *especially* if you're Ricky Martin. Ick.

4) Same goes for scary amounts of chest or back hair. Wax it off, cover it up, or stay at home! It's that simple, gorilla boys.

5) When rubbing sunblock on a friend or significant other, don't get too frisky. We've all seen ladies do the girl-on-girl thing in bars to get attention, and we've all seen couples making out in dark corners, and both

those acts are even *tackier* in broad daylight. Trust me, there are other ways to get people to notice you. I should know.

some burning questions

Running the gossip mill isn't all parties and piña coladas, you know— it's a round-the-clock job. Okay, fine, it's a lot of parties and piña coladas. Maybe I'm not saving lives in the ER, but I'm saving your social lives, people, and that's every bit as important. For those non-believers, I'll share just a few of the questions that keep me up late into the night (when I don't have a party, that is):

Could it be true that **N** has fallen for an older woman? He was last seen waving goodbye to a barely clothed older woman in Hampton Bays. *Interesante.* From what I hear, it wouldn't be the first time . . . Is it also possible that **B** and **S** are exploring their sapphic side—again? Apparently they've taken to nude sunbathing and to sharing a bed. Maybe they've finally made it official!? Will **V** be jealous? I've always wondered about her and that well-groomed buzz cut. Speaking of buzzzzzing, little Ms. **V** was seen taking a late-night swim last night in a less-than-flattering kiddie bathing suit. Keep your eye out for her bumble-bee-on-holiday beach ensemble, coming soon to a beach near you. And then there's **D** . . .

I can't even tell you how many of you have been e-mailing me about tomorrow night's literary salon. Am I missing out? I thought reading Proust in the dark was for skinny, pale boys with coke-bottle glasses, but according to your e-mails, some hottie bookworms are coming out and they're looking for love . . . Could this be the Great Geek Matchup? Well, just because I won't be there doesn't mean I can't help you out. That's just how generous I am. So here you are, by popular request . . .

proper etiquette at a literary salon: dos and don'ts

DO . . . pronounce it properly: it's saaaah-lon, not the place on the corner where all the women have long red nails and you get your hair cut.

DO . . . bring something potent and interesting to drink; that means Pernod, Chartreuse, or ouzo. Leave the Bud at home, thanks.

DO . . . nod along to what everyone says, even if you're too busy checking out the hot poetry nerd across the room to actually listen.

DON'T . . . be totally silent. It's not school—there are no wrong answers—so just make something up to impress people. Or say something in another language. That never fails.

DON'T . . . be inflexible. If fellow members ask you to try something new, remember: truly artistic types are always willing to experiment.

DON'T . . . be surprised if things get heated. Emotions can run high between stanzas.

Okay, kids, have a good time with your books—and let me know how it all turns out. You know I'm curious, and you know what they say about geeks? They're freaks—in bed. Toodles!

You know you love me.

guess v's not in kansas anymore

"Hurry, hurry! Vanessa, hurry up!"

The boisterous four-year-old twins bounced ahead of her, a blur of elbows and curly hair and Brooks Brothers swim trunks with tiny sailboats dotted all over them—Nils in red and Edgar in blue. They ran along the wooded path to the beach, sending a spray of sand into the air.

"Slow down!" Vanessa readjusted the massive pink-and-kelly-green monogrammed canvas tote bag filled with fins and masks, rolled-up Pratesi beach towels, five kinds of sunblock, Bob the Builder activity books, juice boxes, snacks, plastic buckets and shovels, a Frisbee, a soccer ball, and two video iPods loaded with *Little Einsteins* shows. In her other hand, she was holding a massive navy-and-cream striped Smith & Hawken umbrella that Ms. Morgan had insisted she bring along.

"I said, *slow down!*" Vanessa cried again, as the bobbing duo disappeared behind the dune ahead. She was on the verge of screaming her sweaty head off when she decided she really didn't care. *Whatever. Go ahead. Drown. Get kidnapped.*

Fuck if I care. It would be a blessing. The truth was, the twins probably knew the beach as well as they knew their local Central Park playground. It was she who was lost.

She finally reached the crest of the hill and surveyed the scene: Nils and Edgar had vanished into the thicket of bodies crowding the beach, which didn't seem to have one bit of sand available. Tripping in her black All Stars—she'd pulled the laces out and wrongly assumed they'd be every bit as comfortable as flip-flops—Vanessa wove through the maze of blankets, folding chairs, and blond, bronzed twentysomethings with the pale kids they were obviously babysitting. She had exhausted her last reserve of muscle power when she happened upon a four-foot-square patch of beach. *Thank God.* She dropped the overstuffed bag and heavy canvas umbrella onto the burning hot sand, then plopped down.

"Just a lovely day at the beach," she muttered to herself, perfectly mimicking Ms. Morgan's dulcet accent as she dug around in the basket for a blanket, which she half-heartedly spread out in front of her without even standing up. The tote had fallen onto its side but Vanessa didn't bother trying to stuff all the contents back into it. *Stupid, stupid, stupid,* she scolded herself as she realized she'd neglected to bring anything for herself to do. What she'd give to be back in Manhattan, sitting in the cool dark of the Film Forum, watching the latest Todd Solondz movie. Instead she was sitting in the sand, the hot sun beating down on her, with nothing to do but pick the stubborn dried snot globs out of the inside of the twins' tiny nostrils or read the latest issue of *Highlights*.

Reading the labels on the sunblock would actually be more fun.

Vanessa scanned the scene, searching for a flash of the twins' blue or red swim trunks. A few brave nannies waded into the frigid Atlantic surf with the kids they were babysitting, gritting their teeth but laughing. She saw two little boys in swimsuits identical to Nils's and Edgar's and wondered momentarily if anyone at the James-Morgan household would even notice if she brought them home instead.

She'd been in the Hamptons for less than a day, but it was long enough to tell that Ms. Morgan was even less interested than usual in the boys, and that Mr. James Grossman's single check-in phone call was pretty much the daily norm. It was like they were all a bunch of windup robots programmed to perform their own tasks with zero genuine interaction with or feelings about anyone else. Not that Vanessa was a mush, but come on.

It was just eleven in the morning, and the beach belonged to kids and their caretakers. Vanessa studied her peers, the army of au pairs, wondering if maybe she'd strike up a friendship. Did the rest of these babysitters have bosses who undressed in front of them? She imagined the Hamptons must be filled with people like Ms. Morgan, and she wouldn't mind having someone to swap bizarre employer stories with. But looking around, it didn't seem too likely that any of these lithe creatures, with their perfect tans, oversize sunglasses, and manicured nails, would want to have anything to do with her. Or vice versa. Basically, it was like being back at Constance Billard, the school that had tormented her for the last three years.

Vanessa stared out at the endless ocean, suddenly fighting the urge to cry. She kicked her sneakers off and crossed her legs, looking in the mess of things around her for something to drink. She found a tiny box of apple juice and opened the cellophane-wrapped straw, stabbing it into the little hole in the box angrily.

"There you are!" Nils skipped toward her across the sand, taking a shortcut over their neighbors' blankets and towels.

"Don't do that," she scolded him. "Or do and get yelled at. Whatever. Where's your brother?"

"Don't know." He dropped to the ground and rummaged through the stuff that was strewn all over the blanket. "Vanessa, you got sand inside my Cheez-Its."

"Life's rough, sometimes." Vanessa inspected her milk-white ankles and even paler feet. She almost wished she'd thought to get a pedicure. She swiveled them off the blanket and buried them in the sand. "Please, Nils, tell me you didn't kill your brother."

Nils grinned at her, leaned in closer, placing his sticky, sand-covered little hands on her shoulders, and burped in her face.

An overprivileged psychopath in the making.

"The boy you're *supposed* to be watching is over *there*," a familiar whiny voice piped up.

Vanessa turned to meet the cool glare of her old class-mate, Kati Farkas. Kati sported a professionally sprayed–on tan and a too-small black Gucci bikini. Beside her lay her best friend, Isabel Coates. Isabel was on her tummy with her pea green string bikini top off. A tiny redheaded girl was rubbing her back with Bain de Soleil bronzing oil.

"Oh, hello," Vanessa responded coldly. Two other long-limbed mannequin types lounged beside Isabel beneath a pink-and-white striped umbrella. "Are you a nanny for the summer too?" she asked Kati, even though she knew it couldn't possibly be true. Kati and Isabel *work?* Never.

Kati rolled her eyes. "She's my niece. I like watching her. She gets us stuff and rubs on our lotion and guys think she's cute."

Vanessa nodded. She really had no response. Then she caught sight of Edgar across the beach, walking to the edge of the water and then screaming excitedly every time a frothy wave crashed at his feet. She was about to stand and grab him, but he saw her and started to run toward her instead. She turned back to Kati. "Thanks for the tip," she said a little sarcastically. Maybe if she asked both twins to rub her with oil, she'd be thronged by hot Hamptons surfer boys— just her type. Right.

"Nice suit," Isabel piped up meanly.

Vanessa knew she looked ridiculous in Jenny's girls' size 12 Hanna Andersson bumble-bee-striped bathing suit, but she could hardly resist the urge to kick sand in Isabel's eyes. Instead she finished her juice box in one guttural slurp.

She heard the skinny girls lying next to Isabel snicker. Assholes. She was about to offer them an icy death-glare when she suddenly realized she knew them! Except . . . *not.* At first the girls looked exactly like Blair and Serena, but then the longer she stared at them, the more deformed they appeared. The brunette had a shaggy face-framing haircut and brilliant blue eyes, and two enormous teeth protruding from between her lips. The blonde, who was frighteningly skinny, was almost beautiful except for the visible pulsating purple-blue vein in her forehead and the fact that one of her nearly navy-colored eyes was slightly lopsided. Plus, a truly beautiful girl like Serena wouldn't be caught dead in a purple cutout bathing suit like the one this girl had on. There was even a ridiculous cutout hole on her belly button.

Still, for that split second, a wave of relief had washed over her. Friends! She could have real, human friends out here! It made her realize: even if these low-rent versions weren't the real thing, Blair and Serena *must* be kicking around somewhere, right? Where else would those two go for the summer?

"Do you haff a problem?" The weird impostor Blair glared at Vanessa. "Maybe is something I can help you with?"

"Oh, sorry," Vanessa stammered, embarrassed that she'd been caught staring. "It's just that—"

"Yes?" the girl demanded bitchily.

"It's just that you reminded me of someone I know." Was this girl Russian or just retarded?

"Mmmm." Bizarro Blair studied Vanessa closely. Then skankbomb blond version of Serena sitting to her right leaned over and whispered something into Bizarro Blair's ear, dramatically.

How friendly.

"You know vhat?" Bizarro Blair smiled at Vanessa and ran her fingers through her thick, shoulder-length chestnut hair. "You give me very good ideas."

"Vhatever." Vanessa turned away from the blanket full of bitches and focused her attention on the twins, who were now taking turns spitting chunks of chewed-up orange cracker at one another.

"Very good idea," the Blair clone repeated behind her.

Oh? And what could *that* be?

d's big fat geek experiment

"You're here!"

Dan peered nervously into the foyer of Greg's sprawling Harlem apartment, where they were holding their very first meeting of the Song of Myself literary salon.

"I'm here." Dan stepped inside, hesitating in the dark foyer, pretending to study a massive oil painting as he anxiously practiced his opening comments in his head. *Welcome everyone, to our first meeting. I'd like to begin by quoting the poet Wallace Stevens, who of course had much to say on the subject of the centrality of literature to the human condition . . . "Let be be finale of seem. The only emperor is the emperor of ice cream."*

"Everything okay?"

The weight of Greg's hand on his shoulder startled Dan. "Hey, sorry."

Greg laughed. "Nervous?"

"No, no," Dan lied. "Just looking at this painting." He gestured at the huge canvas hanging over the mantel in Greg's parents' apartment. They were older than Rufus and spent most of their time in Phoenix. A swirl of glossy grays and flesh tones glinted in the afternoon sunlight streaming through dusty living room windows.

"You like it?" Greg wondered. "It's one of mine."

"Really?" Dan turned to study the painting, actually looking at it this time. When he took a step back into the foyer, and then another, he realized that he had been staring at a life-size self-portrait of Greg, sitting on top of a tiny stepladder, completely naked. "Oh, right." He tittered nervously. "Of course. Yeah. It's you."

"In all my glory." Greg noticed the rectangular-shaped bottle that Dan was gripping as though his life depended on it. "You brought something!"

"Yeah, some absinthe." It was the most literary thing he could find. The kind of thing Rimbaud or Shelley might have drunk. Plus, it was the only unopened bottle in the musty cracked-glass dentist's cabinet his dad stored liquor in.

"Awesome!" Greg took the bottle. "Should I fix us a drink before everyone gets here?"

"Sure." Dan followed his host down the bookshelf-lined hallway toward the living room. "I could use a little something to loosen me up."

Just a little though, right? That stuff is so strong it's like . . . illegal.

"There's shlomeone, I mean, someone, there's . . ." Dan slurred. His tongue felt like it was the size of an eggplant. "Doorbell, dude. They're here. It's time!" he added, attempting to sit up.

"It's time!" Greg leapt up off the low brown leather couch

that he and Dan had been sinking further and further into the more shots of absinthe they drank. They'd allotted an hour for planning their opening remarks, but they'd spent most of the time pouring absinthe over lumps of sugar, then swallowing the sticky, sweet mix in one gulp. Dan picked up the sterling absinthe spoon they'd been sharing and popped it into his mouth.

Taste of metal on my tongue. Poison the color of envy—
I'm delirious, you're delicious, I'm deluded and delusional.
I'm lost without you. I need you.

Dan grinned. It was true—absinthe *did* inspire. He teetered a little as he crossed the living room's shiny wood floors to retrieve his backpack, where his notebook waited for him. He had to get that fragment down on paper before he forgot it.

"Look who's here," Greg called. Dan dropped the bag— poetic fragment already forgotten—and tried to focus on the faces of the people who were streaming into the room, which suddenly seemed to be spinning. Because they'd sent their pictures he felt like he'd met them already. There was the cute Charlotte Brontë girl. And the insane vampire-lover.

"Everyone grab a drink." Greg pointed: "Bar's over there. Plenty more ice in the fridge. Then I guess we can all just sit in a circle and introduce ourselves. Sound good to you, Dan?"

Dan nodded, suddenly unable to form a single word. *Sit.* Yes, that sounded like a good idea. He lurched through the surprisingly thick crowd—just how many people had been at the door? Or had the doorbell rung more than once? How long had he been digging around in his bag for that note-book, anyway? He collapsed back onto the leather couch.

"How about another?" Greg pointed at the silver tray set with a tiny bottle of pale green liquid and a bowl of sugar cubes. Then he took off his glasses, and Dan noticed for the first time that Greg had millions of tiny freckles all over his face.

"But . . . my speech," Dan murmured. "I need to—"

"You need to calm down." Greg gently pried the sterling spoon from Dan's hand and balanced it on the rim of the glass. He deposited a sugar cube on the spoon and poured a thin stream of the potent green liquor over it.

"That was in my mouth," Dan protested.

"Doesn't bother me." Greg grinned, and then used the spoon to give the liquor a quick stir before popping it between his lips. He pulled the spoon out of his mouth and slipped it back into Dan's.

Ew, thanks for the germs!

Greg slipped off his beaten black leather Doc Martens, then stepped up onto the couch, almost stepping on Dan's thigh as he did so. He shook the ice in his glass to get the attention of the assembled company. "Okay, everyone, grab your drinks and settle in. We've got a lot to cover tonight."

The room was filled with voices, but Dan was having trouble focusing his hearing. He was grateful Greg seemed to have everything under control.

"I'll hand the reins over to our other fearless leader now." Placing one hand on Dan's shoulder to steady himself, Greg hopped off the couch and took a seat on the battered wooden floor at Dan's feet.

"Thank you, Greg." Dan wobbled a little as he studied the group. *This is it. This is our salon. And you're their Gertrude Stein.* "Gadies and lentlemen, welcome to our first meeting of our first salon of the inaugural meeting of our group." He burped quietly. "I'm so pleased to excite you and tell you about exciting and books. These things I believe and you believe and we all believe together that about books and books are good and change our lives and make us happier. And it matters to us, doesn't it? It really does."

Dan paused. The only sounds besides the clink of ice were a couple of muffled titters from across the room. His tongue felt thick and dry and he knew he was having trouble with his pronunciation, but he was determined to get his opening remarks out. He'd spent so long drafting their mission statement and fielding e-mails and had gone through revision after revision of his speech—he wasn't going to go and blow it just because he'd had one drink too many.

One?

"We were going to start today with the reading from the book that I liked that I found that day at the Strand. That's where I work. Where's that book? Greg, do you know where I left that book?"

"Hey, hey." Greg laughed. "Why don't we put off the reading for now and maybe just go around the circle or something? We can all introduce ourselves. Dan and I have been reading your e-mails, but we're looking forward to a chance to get to know you guys in real life." Greg helped ease Dan back into his seat on the couch. "Why don't you go first?" He nodded at a girl sitting cross-legged on the floor near the coffee table. Her head was half-shaven and she was sporting a tattoo of a cockroach on her skull. She seemed to have a very toned body, but her face looked weirdly misshapen.

The misshapen-faced girl nodded back. "Yo, what's going

on, my name's Penny," she barked. "Favorite book, totally got to be *Sexing the Cherry*, you know how it goes. I just finished school, heading out to Smith in the fall, but I'm so psyched to be here right now, meeting some cool booklovers, you know?" She turned to glance at the strawberry redhead to her left, who was hugging her knees and sipping shyly at a cup of cheap white wine.

"H-h-hey," strawberry-head whispered. "I'm Susanna. My favorite book is *The Awakening*. I'm from the East Village, I'm thinking of going to Bennington when I finish school next year, and I love Tori Amos."

"You totally look like her," interjected Penny.

Susanna blushed, looking down at the ground.

"I guess I'll go next," blurted out a gaunt guy who looked about fourteen, dressed in a gray suit complete with bright maroon bow tie and sitting in a rocking chair across from Dan.

"Yes, please do," replied Greg, slipping Dan a bottle of water.

Mister Considerate!

"I'm Peter, I'm about to start my sophomore year at NYU, and my favorite writer is definitely J. D. Salinger. In fact, as my honors thesis, I'm thinking of memorizing *Raise High the Roofbeam, Carpenters* in its entirety."

Dan sipped the bottle of tepid water. That sounded vaguely familiar—he sort of remembered having read an e-mail from a devoted Salinger fan, but for some reason he was having trouble remembering things.

Like his own name?

"Anyway," Peter continued, "I'm glad I made the cut. Word on the blogs is that this group is pretty exclusive."

"I heard that too!" exclaimed the girl sitting next to him, a prim brunette whose milk-white face was framed by perfect brown ringlets. "And I'm so lucky that you were willing to include two Salinger enthusiasts. My name is Franny, and yes, I'm named after the Salinger book, and yes, it's obviously my favorite book in the world. I'll be starting at Vassar next year and, um, well, I guess I hope I make some new friends today."

Maybe she'll meet her Zooey?

"Vanessa," Dan murmured, running his hands over the soft-prickly stubble on the back of her head as she kissed him ever so tenderly. "You came back to me."

"Er, Dan? It's me, Greg. Are you okay?"

Greg's voice snapped Dan back to reality. He sat up and rubbed his eyes. "Oh, sorry, I think I was nodding off there."

"It's okay. You've been sleeping for about an hour."

"I have?" He stood up and then sat down again quickly. Whoa. "I was just listening to that girl talk about liking Salinger and that's the last thing I remember . . ."

"That girl?" asked Greg, pointing out the curly-haired Franny, who was sprawled on the floor across the room while Peter, her fellow Salinger fan, tickled her neck with his tongue. "She, uh, connected with a fellow book lover, as you can see."

"What's going on?" Dan looked around the room, which had grown considerably darker. It seemed like all twenty-two salon-goers were hunkered on the floor in pairs, or in small groups. No one seemed to be doing much talking, and if they were, it certainly wasn't about books. On the room's other big couch, Dan counted seven legs and eight arms. The half-bald punk girl, Penny, was getting her multiply pierced ears worked over lovingly by that redhead Susanna's tongue right in front of him. Dan frowned. His elite literary gathering was turning into an *orgy*. And he could have sworn someone had been kissing him right before he woke up. But who? There weren't any girls there with completely shaved heads.

"Don't worry, Dan," murmured Greg, slipping an arm around his shoulders. "We're all just having a good time getting to know one another. You know, it's like we wanted, right?"

Dan nodded. It *was?*

Greg reached out and cupped Dan's chin gently with his hand. "We're all passionate people, passionate about books, passionate about life." Squeezing Dan's chin playfully, Greg pulled Dan's face close to his and kissed him, softly, on the lips.

Dan yanked his face away. Excuse me? *What the fuck?*

Greg smiled and kissed Dan again, this time letting his warm tongue slip over Dan's lips. Dan was about to pull away again, but his hand involuntarily ran up the back of Greg's neck and into his short, prickly hair. There was something so totally familiar and comforting about kissing someone with short, spiky hair.

Hello? Even if that someone is a dude?

Feeling totally confused and extremely nauseated all of a sudden, Dan mustered enough energy to push Greg away and mumbled something about needing to puke as he stumbled for the bathroom. It was the absinthe that was to blame, he assured himself as he settled onto the white-tiled floor in front of the toilet.

For the kissing-someone-with-face-stubble part, or the puking part?

Air Mail - Par Avion - July 11

Hi Dan!

How come you haven't been replying to my postcards?
Are you okay? Has Vanessa painted my room black yet?
Write me baaaaack!

Love (but not for long if you don't write me soon),

Jenny

s and b's sweet revenge

"Are you ready yet?" Serena banged on the thick, bleached wood sliding door to the guest house's only bathroom, straining her voice to be heard over the persistent beat of techno playing outside, and the noise of partygoers laughing and yelling to one another across the wide, emerald green lawn.

"Almost." Blair dabbed a bit of her current favorite perfume—a lilac concoction from Viktor & Rolf—behind her earlobes, on her wrists, and, just in case, on the soft space between her breasts that was just visible in her low-cut, tissue-weight pale yellow cotton Alberta Ferretti dress. She glanced at herself in the mirror, imagining what she might look like if someone like, say, Nate, just happened to wander next door to check out the party. With her tousled, beachy hair and her long nearly white dress, she looked like a bride about to get married on a sailboat. A sailboat like the *Charlotte*, the boat Nate had built that very first summer they were together.

Which was the only sailboat she'd ever really sailed on.

She'd been thinking about Nate a lot ever since they ran into him three days ago, hoping he'd come visit again. She'd already heard from a million people that his hot romance or whateverthefuck he had with that townie girl was long over, and with some proper groveling, she could forgive him for his romantic retardation. Yes, he was a total fuckup and yes, he'd broken her heart a million times, but something about the way he'd watched her run off, taking in her familiar naked form like it was a painting or something, had left her wanting to see him again and again.

Spinning around on the heels of her white alligator Bailey Winter gladiator sandals, Blair slid the rolling bathroom door open dramatically and stepped into the bedroom, where Serena was pretending to smoke the fourth cigarette she'd lit since Blair first disappeared into the bathroom.

Boredom can turn any nice girl into a pyromaniac.

"Nice choice." Serena nodded approvingly, studying Blair's outfit. "But we've got to make our grand entrance soon, and there's no way I'm doing it without you."

"You-know-who already outside?" Blair asked.

Serena hopped off the bed and walked over to peer out the window at the action poolside. Blair joined her, taking in the dozens of silhouettes and the bright blue pool lit up behind them. She spied Ibiza and Svetlana in the distance. "DJ booth." Serena pointed. "Nice shorts," she added, pretending to admire Ibiza's trashy, butt-cheek-revealing hot pants.

Blair snorted, stepping back inside the bathroom to dab a bit of her Aesop nail cream onto her cuticles—they seemed a little dry lately.

Must be all that manual labor.

"Shit, Blair, come on, what are you doing back in the bathroom?"

"I'm coming, I'm coming." Blair wiped the excess cream off her nails with one quick swipe. She dropped the tissue in the trash and froze. What. The. Fuck. What was that in the trash!? She bent over and picked up the mother-of-pearl-encrusted basket and placed it on the rose-marble counter-top. "Get in here."

"You look *fine*." Serena leaned into the bathroom to grab Blair's forearm. "Let's just go. I'm dying for a drink."

"Look." Blair shook the basket angrily. "Does this strike you as at all suspicious?"

Serena glanced at the baby-pink plastic bottle inside the trash can. "Nair." She paused. "Whatever. I mean, I prefer a waxing, but who knows what they do in Latvia or wherever."

"There's something weird going on." Blair's eyes darted all over the bathroom, looking for signs of criminal activity. She felt like Audrey Hepburn in *Charade*. She just *knew* she was in danger. She could *sense* it. Of course! It dawned on her at last, and she threw open the creamy linen shower curtain, sending its sleek gold hanging rings clattering.

"What's going on?" Serena yawned, smoothing the waist of her Chloé micropleated cotton sundress.

"I know they're up to something." Blair grabbed her bottle of Kerastase shampoo from the shelf in the shower. "And I know it can't possibly be anything original. And I think we both know that the Nair-in-the-shampoo thing is the most obvious trick in the world. Remember that time? At Isabel's sleepover? When we were, like, eleven?"

Serena just stared at her.

"Well, *I* remember." Blair unscrewed the top of the bottle. She didn't even need to sniff it to realize that someone had indeed tried to pull a switch on her—the powerful chemical fart stench of the depilatory was unmistakable. "Bitches!" she swore. "It's a fucking good thing I wanted to have beach hair." She touched her brown locks worriedly to make sure they were still there. "Now it's fucking *war.*"

Dignified and determined, Blair and Serena burst out of the guest house's French doors and onto the white pebble path leading to the swimming pool. Blair surveyed the crowd, seeing now that they were all men. Every single one. *Whoa.* A hundred, maybe a hundred and fifty people, and the only girls in sight were her and Serena—and Ibiza and Svetlana, of course.

"My dad would *totally* love this." Blair almost wished that her fabulous gay dad, Harold Waldorf, and his much-younger French boyfriend, Etienne or Edouard or whateverthefuck his name was, weren't off living the good life in the south of France. She wanted someone besides Serena to witness what was about to happen.

"My girls are here!" Bailey Winter emerged from a thicket of silver-haired news-anchory types, all of whom seemed to be wearing blue blazers and white pants, despite the fact that it was easily eighty degrees. Bailey himself wore a similar ensemble, but with three-quarter-length sleeves and pant legs that left his neon-orange-and-hot-pink argyle knee socks and white nubuck saddle shoes exposed. Skipping up the path to Blair and Serena, he extended one chubby hand to each of them, his entourage of five yelping pugs following closely on his heels.

"Come, girls, make a Bailey sandwich." He giggled. "Hopefully it won't be the only threesome I'm in tonight." He grinned and gave a little wave to the shirtless DJ.

"Lovely party," Blair complimented Bailey, noticing the many barely clothed waiters circulating with champagne flutes.

"Thank you, darling!" Bailey squealed. "Step, step, ladies. We need to get you some drinks!" He dashed off in the direction of the bar, pulling the two along with him like puppies on a leash. "Bartender!" he barked at the golden surfer-boy model-type who was behind the bar. His uniform, like those of the rest of the waitstaff, consisted of a low-cut Bailey Winter Garçon cotton-and-cashmere vest over his perfectly defined bare chest.

"What do my pets want?" Bailey cooed.

"Two Negronis." Blair turned to scan the crowd, a blur of white trousers against the green grass, perfect haircuts and impressive muscles peeking out of too-short sleeves.

Then she spotted them: Ibiza and Svetlana, clad in white. Copycat bitches. Svetlana wore a tacky, stretchy asymmetrical dress that emphasized her basically nonexistent chest. Ibiza had squeezed herself into a backless white hot pants jumpsuit that looked like something Blair's mother might have worn to Studio 54, like, thirty years ago. Nasty.

Why not do something about it then?

"Here you are." The bartender handed Blair two tumblers filled with the rich, orange liquid. "I'm Gavin."

"Thank you, Gavin." Serena batted her eyelashes at him. "So . . . are you out here all summer?" she asked, leaning against the weathered-wood bar.

"Not now," Blair snapped, grabbing her friend's arm. She

had no patience for Serena's flirting—not when they had a job to do.

"Sorry." Serena took a small sip of the bittersweet cocktail. "I was just having a little fun. He's probably the only nongay guy here."

"Bailey, I'd like to get a closer look at the DJ booth," Blair announced.

"Oh, honey, you read my *mind*." Bailey guided the two by their elbows around the perimeter of the pool toward the pink-trimmed white cabana that had been erected for the occasion. "He's positively scrumptious, don't you think? Oh, shoo, girls." He waved away Ibiza and Svetlana, who were pawing through the milk crates packed with records. "He's got *work* to do!"

"Ve're helping him," Ibiza protested, pouting and sipping at her chardonnay.

"Sure you are." Bailey winked sarcastically at Blair.

"Why don't we all go over there and chat?" Blair pointed at an all-white seating area next to the pool.

"Yes, yes, you girls go sit—I mean, I had those cushions specially made just for this party. That is the most divine bleached Italian silk. Very rare. Very special. So lounge, come on, look pretty. Go on, run along." Bailey raised his tiny Tiffany champagne flute in salute. "I'll stay here and keep an eye on our music man, don't you worry!"

Ibiza and Svetlana arranged themselves on the overstuffed, raw-silk pillows stationed poolside. Blair and Serena stood above them, grimacing.

"He's a gay, you do know?" Ibiza sipped her wine and stared coldly at Blair.

Blair looked down at her. It was almost like looking in a particularly fucked-up trick mirror at a carnival. "Yes, I'm aware, thanks."

"I just thought, you know, you hold hands with him, I tell you, you know, don't expect anything to happen," Ibiza continued.

"Why would I expect anything to happen?" Blair looked blankly at Serena.

"I don't know." Serena shrugged.

"I mean, what could happen?" Blair smiled, then suddenly tripped spastically forward. Her still-untouched deep-orange cocktail flew at Ibiza's chest. She grabbed Serena's arm to steady herself, which caused Serena's drink to spill all over Svetlana's head.

What are the odds?

The crowd clustered around the quartet gave a collective, horrified gasp as everything—the white dresses, the white pillows, Svetlana's white-blond hair—turned a deep tangerine color right before their eyes.

"Oh goodness, what have I done?" Blair used her white-and-cream striped cocktail napkin to dab delicately at the front of Ibiza's dress.

"Ees ruined, you beetch. Is Versace!" Ibiza waved her away irritably.

"What happened?" Bailey Winter dashed toward them, palms pressed against his cheeks in dismay. His five pugs barked uneasily at the crowd. "What's going on? Someone spilled? Oh my word! My *pillows!*"

"They do this!" barked Ibiza, the tangerine stain spreading across her hideous formerly white jumpsuit. Between the stain and her brassy highlights and too-orange tan, she was beginning to look like a clementine-colored Oompa Loompa. "They do on purpose!"

"We better go get some towels . . ." Blair backed away from the scene and into the still-stunned-silent crowd.

"Towels." Serena nodded seriously. She pulled at her own white-blond locks, tying the ends in a knot to hold them in place.

"I need a minute alone, please!" Bailey Winter raised his hands and started shooing. "Everyone, please, just back to the party. Pretend I'm not here."

That's right: ignore the weeping man in neon argyle surrounded by barking dogs.

"We'll give you a minute." Blair grabbed Serena's hand and pulled her through the crowd of men. By the time they reached the lawn, both of them were nearly hysterical with giggles.

"What now?" Serena gasped. "We can't go back there."

Blair dropped her crystal-cut tumbler to the ground, where it landed with a thud. "Can we make it over this?" She stood on her tiptoes to more closely examine the redwood fence that separated the Winter estate from the Archibald residence.

Of course you can. In heels.

"Definitely." Serena placed her glass on the spongy grass and pulled herself up onto the fence.

Blair followed her, easily maneuvering her body over the fence and landing on the grassy lawn beyond it. She inspected her pale yellow dress—there was a stain across the bodice from where she'd touched the fence. "Bollocks," she swore.

No pain, no gain.

"Blair? Serena?"

Blair looked up from her ruined dress to find exactly who she'd secretly hoped to find in the Archibalds' yard.

"Hello, Nate." She tucked her hair behind her ear and smiled.

"I heard someone scream. I thought it was a wild animal or something." Nate looked dazed, like he'd been napping.

Or smoking, more likely.

"I was worried about you guys," he went on.

"That's sweet," Blair cooed, reaching out to take Serena's hand. "Now take us home."

"What do you mean?" Nate blinked, staring at them like he was still trying to figure out if they were real or just an apparition. "Home, *here?* Of course. Come on in—"

"No, *home!*" Blair and Serena shrieked in unison. Then they took off running across the perfectly trimmed lawn toward the driveway, where Nate's father's pride and joy, a hunter green Aston Martin convertible, sat basking in the cool night air.

Road trip!

it's all about timing

"Well, well, well, look what the hairless cat dragged in." Chuck Bass slid his titanium Christian Roth sunglasses down his nose and fired a crooked smile at Vanessa. She'd barely taken two steps into Bailey Winter's expansive yard before Chuck had stepped into her path and started clucking at her. His pet snow monkey, Sweetie, was perched on his shoulder, wearing a sequined sailor outfit, bobbing up and down on its hind legs and tugging at the collar of Chuck's pale pink Hugo Boss polo. It occurred to Vanessa that Sweetie was quite possibly using it as toilet paper.

"Oh, hey, Chuck." She vaguely remembered that this guy was bad news—Dan didn't like him for some reason, and she'd heard people gossip about him, although you couldn't ever really trust that.

Is that a fact?

"You just missed the show, honey." Chuck popped his polo collar back into place and smiled insinuatingly. "Blair and Serena, up to their old tricks."

"Thank God they're here." Vanessa released an audible

sigh of relief. After all, she'd come specifically to see them, following a hot tip from the nanny next door, a svelte Irish girl named Siobhan who, despite being a servant like Vanessa, seemed to be at the center of the Hamptons social scene. She felt moderately self-conscious about her outfit—actual black capri pants that she hadn't just cut off herself and a simple black cotton shell she'd bought at Club Monaco just before leaving for Amagansett—but she figured it would be okay since her friends were here.

"They *were,* darling." Chuck was distractedly checking his text messages. "You totally missed it. Hurricane Blair left some real damage in her wake."

Behind him the scene was pandemonium: a deeply tanned near-midget was kneeling by the edge of the swimming pool crying hysterically, while a thick crowd of gorgeous gay men moved further and further away from him. Standing nearby, in the middle of some orange-splattered white pillows, were two very familiar girls. "But isn't that—"

"Blair and Serena? Don't be fooled, darling. Total impostors. Look closely." Chuck went back to texting in his BlackBerry.

Vanessa looked again and realized that Chuck was right—the brunette and blonde she'd first taken for Blair and Serena were not quite as pretty or healthy-looking as the originals. The fact that their once-white outfits were both marred by sloppy, barfy-looking stains further cemented it. She squinted at them, realizing they were the faux versions she'd seen on the beach only hours before.

Just what she needed—a reminder of her horrible afternoon with the terror twins. The rest of their time at the beach had been uneventful enough, but the moment they returned to the house, Ms. Morgan had dug into her about what SPF she'd used on the boys, what books they'd read, and how she'd really prefer Vanessa not ruin their dinner with Cheez-Its. Vanessa had nodded patiently, then raced to her upstairs room and quickly changed into something relatively presentable. Then she'd dashed out of the house and into the night, refusing to let the minor fact that she didn't have either a driver's license or a car get in her way. She'd grabbed one of the twins' tiny bicycles from the hook from which it was suspended and pedaled toward civilization, figuring that it would only be a matter of time before she came across someone who could direct her to where Blair and Serena might be. Luckily, she'd bumped into Siobhan after about one block.

"Do you know where they went?" Vanessa turned to see Chuck Bass disappearing into the crowd, his hand raised high above his head to avoid spilling his drink.

Great. No Blair, no Serena, and now, no Chuck. Vanessa had a vision of herself alone, shivering on the beach, trying to avoid the perverts and murderous models.

Just another night in East Hampton.

Well, there's only one cure for a lonely night, Vanessa reasoned as she dove into the crowd, slipping through a trio of shirtless musclemen, making a beeline for—where else?— the bar.

"Vodka martini." She smiled at the bartender, giving him her best yes-I'm-on-the-guest-list look. She almost never drank, but holding a martini might give her a new outlook on life.

The bartender went right to work and smoothly handed

over a glass. Clutching the stem, Vanessa turned back into the crowd, unsure who to talk to. There was Chuck, laughing as he made small talk with a very tall man, and there were the two impostors from the beach, frowning and pathetically dabbing at their stained outfits with damp napkins.

Tough choice.

Vanessa wove through a thicket of linen-pants-clad types, heading toward the edge of the pool. "We meet again," she offered by way of introduction. "I'm Vanessa."

The blond girl stared at her dumbly through her tear-blurred slightly crossed eyes.

"You again." The faux Blair glared at her. "We must go change." The girl grabbed her friend's hand and started walking away from Vanessa. "Maybe you should also change."

Vanessa resisted the urge to pitch her drink at the girl's bucktoothed face.

Sliding off her flip-flops, she took a seat and dangled her feet into the aqua-colored water. She sipped her martini nervously, trying to drink her way through that horrible I'm-at-a-party-and-no-one-is-talking-to-me shame. Then she glanced at her watch, fiddled with her outfit, and stared at the placid surface of the swimming pool, pretending to be engrossed in each task.

"Yooo-hooo. Excuse me, dear."

Had someone called security?

Vanessa turned oh-so-casually to come face-to-face with Bailey Winter himself, the gaytastic designer she'd crossed paths with on the set of *Breakfast at Fred's* the day before she was excommunicated, and the host of the party she just happened to be crashing.

"Hi!" She smiled enthusiastically, hoping to make him forget he hadn't invited her to his soirée.

"Oh dear." The designer produced a floral-printed silk hankie from the breast pocket of his navy blue linen blazer and dabbed at his red eyes with the tip of it. "I'm all at sixes and sevens. My cushions, you see—they're ruined."

Vanessa frowned at the booze-stained ivory cushions perched at the edge of the pool. "That's too bad."

"Oh, every cloud has a silver lining, honey," he announced dramatically, his tears spontaneously drying up. "And dare I say, I think you are positively sterling! Who are you and where did you come from? You're just the most delicious little thing." Still clutching his handkerchief, Bailey Winter reached up and caressed Vanessa's cheek.

Silk and snot. How lovely.

"I'm, um, looking for some friends of mine. Blair and Serena?"

"Yes, those two vixens, well, who knows where they've gone off to—and who cares!" He gripped her upper arm tightly with his small hand. "You're what I've been looking for. You're the new *new* new look. At last!"

"Excuse me?" Vanessa wanted to back away, but if she did, she'd fall into the pool.

"You must stay with me this summer," he continued, enraptured. "Your energy, your profile, your . . . baldness. They're positively inspiring! Say you will, my dear. Spend the night. At least one night. Please. Don't make Uncle Bailey beg."

"Stay here?" Vanessa surveyed the scene once more: a modern glass-and-concrete mansion, a glittering blue pool, hundreds of perfectly dressed and groomed men, chilled martinis—it was like a Fellini film, if Fellini had ever made a movie about summer in the Hamptons. She felt a surge of creativity that almost took her breath away. Of course! A movie, in the Hamptons! An impressionistic documentary, inter-splicing party footage with first-person interviews, documenting the creative process of one of the fashion industry's leading forces. It was a little bit Robert Altman, a little bit *Grey Gardens*. Not to mention that it beat the shit out of booger patrol at the James-Morgans'. "Stay here," she repeated, nodding slowly. "Why, yes. I'd *love* to."

She would?

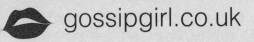 gossipgirl.co.uk

topics ◀ **previous** **next** ▶ **post a question** **reply**

Disclaimer: All the real names of places, people, and events have been altered or abbreviated to protect the innocent. Namely, me.

hey people!

Okay, so I know I already interrupted your regularly scheduled programming for an important message, but this is an *emergency*. I'm putting out an APB—that's all-points-bulletin in case you didn't know—on some of our very favorite people . . .

Missing: A vintage hunter green Aston Martin convertible. Last seen speeding out of Georgica Pond a little after sundown. Reports vary, but my best sources say the car contained at least three people—a guy and two girls—and I'm getting reports that at least one of the girls was wearing white. Could someone be eloping? Please keep your eyes peeled. And now, back to your regularly scheduled dish.

book report

Our first juicy report affirms what I both hoped and feared about those book geeks: they really *are* freaks in bed. Rumor has it that a certain Harlem-based intellectual salon went from swapping literary thought to swapping spit—and fast. Talk about an introductory "getting to know you" meeting. I wonder if that's what **D** and his new friend **G** had in mind when they sought out "like-minded young men and women" and asked applicants to attach their pictures . . . Then again, from what I hear, these eager literati saw beyond the shackles of identity—like, um, gender—and simply embraced the soul (and some other things) of the person next to them. I guess that's what they mean about not judging a book by its cover.

So does this little freak-orgy mean the demise of literary debate? Can people no longer sit around a rambling Harlem apartment and discuss great works of literature without getting frisky? Or does it symbolize the return of freaky group-sex organizations like Plato's Retreat? (Can I just say . . . ew.) Sorry to disappoint, but for once I don't know for sure. I *will* tell you what it means for me, however: I am never, ever going above One-hundredth Street. I don't care how "stimulating" the event promises to be.

paint by numbers

Speaking of parties with an, ahem, same-sex appeal, I have a bone to pick with a certain flamboyant designer about his latest stylish affair: What's with the all-white theme? For people who consider themselves free thinkers, the idea itself is just so . . . single-minded (although maybe I'm just smarting from my exclusion from the party, due to the similarly *single-minded* all-*male* theme). I suppose it's a way for the rich and famous to make themselves feel chic and fabulous—anybody remember that rocker whose Greenwich Village apartment was done entirely in white? Even his guests had to match the décor. And while it may look fantastic for five minutes, it's so impractical—hello, drunk people, colorful drinks, and white sofas? Can anyone else put two and two together? Personally, I'm up for anything colorful, particularly in summer. To prove my point, a few of my favorite (colorful) things: sunset-pink Cosmos, blue-green ocean water, mint chocolate-chip ice cream, and last but not least . . . tan boys in pastel shirts. Talk about a color combination!

your e-mail

Dear the Gossip Girl,
I am beautiful brunette from foreign land so maybe there is somethings I don't understand about America. I ask your help

to explain to me this please: is bald now beautiful? Do American men like girls to look like this? With shaved head? Please advise.

—Confused

 Dear C,

I think you've misunderstood. Bald is beautiful when we're talking about a Brazilian, but most fellows I know like something to run their fingers through. It's the rare woman indeed who can pull off the full-on buzz . . . I've seen it work only once before. Good luck!

—GG

 Dear GG,

I've been in Europe for the summer and am worried about my big brother back in New York. He hasn't replied to any of my postcards, and when I called home a few minutes ago, my dad said he was "on the lam with a bottle of absinthe." Eeek! Do you think he's okay?

—Worried Little Sis

 Dear WLS,

Not to worry! Your bro is probably just out enjoying himself and trying new things. Trust me, that's a good thing. If you're still concerned about his whereabouts, send me his pic . . . If he's cute, I'll track him down for you!

—GG

sightings

N, making his first beach appearance of the season with a friend I hardly recognized—what's up, **A**, you been working out? Great results! I've got the camera-phone pics to prove it. Yum. Two ladies matching the descriptions of **B** and **S** were spotted chewing gum behind a gas station on Main Street, late at night, but let's take that one with a grain of salt, because another report also had **B** and **S** buying depilatories at Long's, and something tells me those girls would never attempt a home job, even in an emergency. I mean, there are experts for that sort of thing, and yes, they make house calls! **V** pedaling around East Hampton on a child's bike with training wheels. Maybe she's making some kind of environmental point? Good for her. **D**'s being a good environmentalist himself, if that was indeed him passed out on the 2 train instead of cabbing it. BTW, **K** and **I**: if you're going to try to crash an all-boy party, it helps immensely if you've got a shaved head and boring unisex outfit. More than a few of our readers spotted you slinking home in your Puccis after you were rejected at the gate. Sorry, girls!

That's enough for now. I'm going to go get to know a new friend of mine—he's a lifeguard and only speaks Dutch—and you've got work to do, anyway: get out there and create some more dirt for me to dish. You know how much I love you for it. And of course . . .

You know you love me.

gossip girl

before sunrise

"Turn it up!" Nate cupped the flame of Serena's dainty silver lighter, trying to light a cigarette as Serena navigated the convertible roadster along the deserted Long Island Expressway.

Best way to beat the summer traffic? Set out in the middle of the night.

His cigarette lit, Nate tossed the lighter back onto the empty passenger seat in front of him. Serena reached over and cranked up the volume as high as it would go, but even that loud, Bob Dylan's distinctive warble was barely audible over the whoosh of wind.

"I'm cold. Can't we put the top up?" Blair wrapped her arms around herself and frowned.

"I don't know how it works," Nate admitted. "But I can help keep you warm if you like." He draped his left arm around her shoulder protectively.

Just like old times.

Blair leaned into the front of the car and grabbed the cardigan Serena had abandoned there. "And I'm *tired.*

Whose bright idea was it to stop for dinner?" She pulled the sweater on and leaned back into the caramel leather upholstery.

It had been Blair's suggestion, actually, that they get dinner. She'd wanted to stop at a diner in Merritt—she and her dad had always stopped there on their family trips to Southampton when she was a kid—but they'd gotten lost, and it had taken an hour and a half just to find it. Nate decided not to remind her of this.

"Maybe you should take a little nap," he suggested.

"We'll be there soon," Serena chimed in from the front seat. "I can almost smell the city."

Nate sniffed at the cool, damp air. He couldn't smell anything but the gritty burn of his cigarette and the honey-almond aroma of Blair's hair. He couldn't see much, either, just the vague outlines of the car and his friends, and the dark void of that along-the-highway wilderness, which was barely illuminated by the thin sliver of summer moon. After a couple of other pit stops—to fill up the tank, to take dorky pictures of the three of them making faces in front of different scenic spots, to stock up on cigarettes and Diet Coke and junk food—they'd managed to waste most of the night. It seemed almost impossible that in a few hours Nate was supposed to climb back on that shitty bicycle and show up at Coach Michaels's house for another day of hard labor and sexual harassment.

Guess he'll be calling in sick. Again.

"So what's our plan, anyway?" Serena glanced over her shoulder and into the backseat. "Where exactly am I driving us?"

"Let's go to the Ritz." Blair hopped up and down in her

seat like a little kid who had to pee. "Let's get a suite and order room service and sleep all day tomorrow."

"How about we go right to the Three Guys coffee shop and we pig out on pancakes?" Serena suggested.

Nate weighed the options: a hotel room shared with Blair and Serena or a greasy early morning breakfast.

Decisions, decisions.

But Nate had his own plan. He'd been going over it in his head for a couple of days now, ever since Anthony told him to seize the day. And now he knew what he wanted: an impromptu summer cruise on his dad's boat. He could just picture it. He'd navigate them out of the New York harbor, the sun rising over the East River. They'd head north, toward the Cape, and eventually toward his parents' place in Mt. Desert Island, Maine. They'd spend the rest of the summer lounging around on the sun-drenched deck in their underwear. They'd dive overboard and splash around in the cool water like kids. They'd pull into small towns so he could stock up on cigarettes and beer and Blair could buy magazines and whatever else she needed. Then, when they'd worked up an appetite from fishing or swimming or making love, he and Blair would raid the fully stocked kitchen, eating artichoke hearts directly out of the jar with their fingers.

Forgetting about someone?

That was the summer he was supposed to be having, and at last, he was seizing the day. The only problem was, well . . . Serena. Never mind that he and Blair weren't quite a couple again. They'd had ups and downs for as long as they'd known each other, but they always came back to the same point: they were supposed to be together. And that point was coming again. That point was on the *Charlotte*. Nate closed his eyes, trying desperately to think of a guy they could bring along on their grand voyage to keep Serena occupied while he worked on winning back Blair. Jeremy? Anthony? Nah, she was out of their league.

He flicked his cigarette out of the car and cleared his throat. "I've got it," he announced. "Let's get the *Charlotte*. Then we'll just, like, sail away."

"Awesome!" Serena took both hands off the wheel and clapped them together. "Natie, you're a genius!"

"I don't know." Blair sat up. "I kind of just feel like taking a shower and going to bed."

Blair fidgeted in her seat, her knee brushing against Nate's. Was she doing that on purpose? It sent a palpable surge of electricity through his body. He felt more clear-headed and aware than he had in months. It was like everything that had happened to him lately—getting in trouble and almost not graduating, getting shipped off to slave labor in the Hamptons, having that weird short-lived romance with Tawny—had been leading him right here, to this moment. Never mind that he was going to bail on work in a matter of hours, never mind that he had stolen his father's prized possession, never mind that he might not get his diploma—he was with Blair, and when they were together it was like everything else in the world was just . . . *right*.

"There's a shower on board," Serena reminded Blair, picking up her vibrating and blinking Nokia from her lap. "Don't be a baby," she called over her shoulder. "Hello?" she answered her cell phone. Who the hell was calling at four in the morning?

"Hey Serena. How are you? It's Jason. You know, your downstairs neighbor at the town house on Seventy-first Street?"

Serena smiled quietly at the road. Blair was so not expecting this call.

"Hey!" She responded in her friendliest, most upbeat voice. Jason was cute but totally forgettable. After the *Breakfast at Fred's* wrap party, that's exactly what both girls had done—forgotten about him. But Serena wasn't the girl Jason had had the hots for, anyway. "I guess you want to talk to Blair." She shifted into fourth gear around a tight curve in the road.

"Kind of," Jason admitted.

"Hold on." Serena tossed her phone behind her, accidentally hitting Blair in the nose.

Blair had been happily ensconced in one of her epic movielike reveries starring herself and Nate naked on a beach in St. Barts, kissing on the sand while the waves splashed over their bodies, exactly like Deborah Kerr and Burt Lancaster in *From Here to Eternity*. She took the phone. Probably it was her mother, wondering why there was a $10,000 charge at Tod's on her AmEx.

"Hello?" she said with some annoyance. Nate's leg was so warm against hers. She rested her head on his shoulder, seeking comfort while she prepared to have an extremely annoying conversation. "What is it now, Mom?"

"No, it's me, Jason," a boy's voice responded gruffly on the other end.

Blair lifted her head from Nate's shoulder and held the phone away from her face. *Who?*

She glanced at Nate's profile. He was beginning to nod

off, and she wanted to grab him and slip her hands under his shirt, just to feel his warm skin beneath her fingers.

"Hello? Blair?" Jason's voice squawked out of Serena's phone. Blair snapped the phone shut and tossed it into the passenger seat.

"Blair!" Serena scolded. The two girls giggled, sharing a glance through their reflections in the rearview mirror.

Nate shifted in his seat. "What's so funny?" he mumbled, making them laugh even harder.

Then Blair turned, catching Nate staring right at her. But before he could look away, embarrassed, she let one eyelid fall in the sexiest, most unexpected wink Nate had ever seen. "Can I have a smoke?" she finally asked, gently biting her glistening-pink bottom lip.

"Sure." He dug into his pockets for the pack. *Anything for you.*

Aw.

Sunrise must have happened during the four minutes it took them to speed through the Midtown Tunnel and into the city: the sky was dark purple when Serena steered them into the gaping mouth of the tunnel, and by the time the little roadster emerged on the streets of Manhattan, the sun was up, the cars were honking, and it was already starting to get hot.

Nate tried not to be too obvious about watching Blair, which was hard because she was so close he could smell her, could imagine the weight of her body against his if she happened to nod off to sleep, could conjure the soft feeling of her lips and tongue against his on the off chance they just started making out right there in the backseat.

Stop it. Focus. "Just drive downtown." Nate locked eyes with Serena in the rearview mirror. *Did she know what he was thinking? Did she see something?*

Not that she was uncool enough to say anything.

"Aye, aye, captain." Serena made a wide right onto the FDR Drive that sent Nate and Blair hurling to the left as she did.

"Don't kill us." Blair tucked her wind-whipped hair behind her ears.

"Don't worry." Nate gave her right knee a reassuring squeeze.

Blair looked up at him, her eyes glazed and sleepy but the same brilliant blue they'd always been. She smiled and rested her head on his shoulder, still looking up at him.

Nate grinned back, feeling foolish and a little embarrassed, like he was fifteen again. He lost himself in the sensation of the wind in his hair, the thrum of the road beneath him, the smell of the girl he loved leaning against him. It took ten minutes for Serena to zip through the early morning traffic on the highway, and five minutes of navigating the twisting downtown streets before they reached the docks at Battery Park, where Captain Archibald kept the *Charlotte* docked.

"We're here, kids," Serena announced, playing mommy as she guided the tiny car into a curbside parking spot and turned off the ignition. "Ready to sail?"

Nate opened the door and clambered out of the backseat. He breathed in the mingling scent of traffic and salt water and warm asphalt; it was a mix of everything he loved—the city, especially in the early morning, and the seaside, where he'd spent the happiest weeks of his life. Maybe he'd been cooped up in the tiny backseat for too long, or maybe he was just excited at the thought of the illicit cruise he was about to undertake, but whatever the reason, Nate actually started to run, dodging pedestrians and leaping over a low gate that separated the docks from the street. The rubber soles of his flip-flops thwacked noisily against the ashy wood slats of the dock. His heart was pounding in his ears: it was really, finally happening—the summer was beginning at last. Once he and Blair stepped on board that boat, everything would change.

"Sir? Sir?" A uniformed dockhand was running down the pier toward Nate, waving his hands in the air above his head like bees were attacking him. "This is private property, sir, you're going to have to leave."

"I'm looking for my boat," Nate explained, scanning the forest of masts for its familiar profile. He'd helped his dad build the thing—he'd have known the boat anywhere. "The *Charlotte*. It's around here somewhere. I want to take her out."

"The *Charlotte?*" The dockhand—a college-age kid who seemed cool enough—stared at Nate, clearly confused. "The Archibald boat?"

"Yeah." Nate nodded, glancing behind him: Blair and Serena were perched on the security gate, swinging their legs in the air and laughing at something. "It's my family's boat. Can you give me the slip number?"

"Sorry, man." The dockhand shook his head, slowly. "She's not here. Captain Archibald sailed up to Newport at the beginning of June—he told me he was planning on keeping her there for the season."

Shit. Nate frowned at the dockhand, then looked back at

Blair once more. She was kicking her little tan legs up and down when a sudden gust of wind off the water caused her gauzy dress to flutter up around her waist. Underneath she was wearing pale pink cotton underwear. He could just make out little white polka dots decorating them.

Forget the boat: for now all he wanted was to lie down next to her, hold her hand, and never let go.

the truth comes out . . .
and so does d

"Male. Ball. Male, ball. Male balls."

Dan groaned and flopped over in the soft, once-white, now coffee-and-nicotine-stained sheets of his bed. *Male balls?* Sweating profusely, he rocked his head from side to side.

"You awake in there?" Rufus Humphrey, Dan's boisterous-and-eccentric-editor-of-lesser-known-Beat-poets dad banged on the bedroom door urgently. "Mail call! Mail call! Are you listening?"

"Mail call!" Dan sat upright in bed. *Mail call, you idiot, not male balls.* "I'm awake," he announced, his voice cracking.

"Remind me to tell you about the early bird and the worm sometime!" Rufus stormed into Dan's bedroom purposefully, clad in a typically demented outfit: a pair of carpenter's pants splattered with the same dingy off-white paint that covered the apartment's walls—making them around nineteen years old—and an official *Breakfast at Fred's* crew jacket he must have pilfered from a pile of Vanessa's dirty laundry. It was unzipped, revealing a chest of furry gray hair. He held a massive cardboard box that someone had haphazardly sealed with twine, butcher paper, bubble wrap, and two kinds of tape. The word FRAGILE was scrawled all over the box in five different languages. Rufus dropped the package onto the bed. "You've got mail."

"Jesus." Dan picked up the ungainly box. He could have tossed it into the air, it was so light. "It doesn't feel like there's even anything *inside* here."

"Open it, open it," Rufus urged. "Your sister sent it all this way and the shipping could not have been cheap, so I'm guessing there's something good in there."

"Sure." Dan started tugging at the twine.

"I didn't hear you come in last night." Rufus grinned down at Dan. "Guess your first meeting went pretty well, huh? Stayed up late, debating the merits of the minor Shakespeare plays, did you?"

"Something like that." Dan burrowed through another layer of paper before finally reaching the flaps of the cardboard box. If there had been any discussion at all the previous night, he couldn't remember it. He could barely remember anything except the sensation of Greg's tongue on his, the fuzz of Greg's facial hair against his own stubble.

Eek.

"I remember my old salon days." Rufus perched on the windowsill and watched as his son reached into the depths of the cardboard box. Dan pulled out fistful after fistful of crumpled-up newspaper. "We had some pretty crazy times back then."

"It wasn't so crazy," Dan replied defensively. At last his hand gripped something firm inside the mush of newspaper. Grabbing hold tightly, he pulled on the narrow object until it popped out and the loose cardboard shell fell to the ground, showering balled-up newspaper all over his floor.

Rufus laughed. "Too bad. You kids today. No passion, no guts. I remember back when I was your age, me and some friends, we'd go out to the lakes, up in New England. Camp out, write poetry, stay up all night talking."

Dan half-listened as he pondered the object in his hands: it was about two feet long and wrapped tightly in a cocoon of bubble wrap and packing tape. He dug at the wrapping with his fingernail, anxiously going over the events of the night before. How far had he gone with Greg exactly? How had he gotten back home? He had almost no memory of putting himself to bed. And he'd woken up in just his favorite pair of red Gap boxer shorts—had he been wearing them yesterday? He couldn't remember.

Rufus had a faraway look in his eye as he continued: "I remember this one afternoon, out on the lake, things got pretty heated. We were all out skinny-dipping and I had this very passionate argument with Crews Whitestone—you know, the playwright. We were arguing about the elemental nature of truth, and things just got so heated, wouldn't you know it, before long there we were, rolling around on the beach, wrestling one another to the ground, each trying to get the other to admit that his conception of the truth was the superior one."

Dan was only half-listening to his dad's pornographic mumblings. He'd found a gap in the bubble wrap and unwound it from the long, ceramic . . . thing.

"Yeah, your literary get-togethers today are probably much more dignified, aren't they?" Rufus went on. "But that's how we liked it then: naked, vibrant, fighting it out over the truth. God, those were the days."

Still trying to tune out his dad, Dan tossed the excess wrapping aside and considered the vessel in his hands: it was a long, hollow, tapered column of white ceramic, finished in a soft, inviting glaze. It was about eighteen inches tall, and open at the top, so it must have been a vase. At the base were two small, rounded pieces, one on either side, which helped stabilize the tall, central shaft. It was a vase. It was something. It was . . . well, a nicely glazed penis.

This was his sister's idea of a present? He put the vase—or whatever it was—on his bedside table and eyed it warily.

"Well, I'd recognize that anywhere." Rufus chuckled, interrupting his reminiscence. He picked up the vase and stroked it gently. "You know who made that, don't you? Your mother. That's her handiwork."

"Really?" Dan took the vase back from his father and studied it more carefully. Maybe he was mistaken: maybe it resembled a rocket ship in flight, or an alien, or maybe it was an abstract representation of an earth mother flanked on either side by her children.

Nope. No matter how he squinted at it or turned his head, it just looked like a big wang.

He turned the vase over to study the base, where he found a tiny, hand-carved inscription: "A totem for my son. Imparted with love."

A *totem*? What the hell did that mean? Was his mother trying to tell him something, something about himself that he'd somehow never managed to figure out before? He hadn't seen his mom in years, and then this—a penis-shaped vase coincidentally shows up in the mail just hours after he'd made out with a guy? But he wasn't gay. How could he be gay? He loved girls. He had loved Serena van der Woodsen. He had loved Bree. And he had loved Vanessa most of all.

Right: the girl who looks like a boy.

Was it possible that he was gay and that everyone but him had known it all along? Was he one of those obviously gay little boys who like to have tea parties with their stuffed animals and carry their mothers' old cast-off purses to school?

Sighing as he placed the vase on the floor by his bed, Dan looked up at his dad, who was lost in thought. "So, you were telling me about the skinny-dipping and the literary discussion." Dan paused. "Was that like, um, normal? For your literary conversations to end up . . . with you, like, naked with some other guy?"

"Normal!" Rufus laughed heartily. "Believe me, when it comes to literature there's nothing more normal. Passion. Fire. When you're young, you're just filled with it. It's got to play out somehow."

Dan nodded, brow furrowed. "So you're saying that, in your experience, it's not uncommon for a literary salon to turn into a naked same-sex orgy?"

"More common than you think, sonny." Rufus ruffled his son's mussed bed-head affectionately. "Too bad times have changed."

Yeah, too bad.

truth—stranger than fiction after all

"Turn your head now, just to the left a tiny centimeter . . . Another centimeter . . ." Vanessa complied, turning her head slightly to the left to allow Bailey Winter an unfettered look at her profile.

"My goodness, isn't that just yummy?" Bailey was talking to no one in particular as he scribbled furiously in his crocodile-bound sketchbook, wielding his pencil and turning the pages like a madman. "Yes, yes, Vanessa, my dear, this is it, you've really got it. You give Giselle and Kate and those little chickadees a run for their money now, don't you, dearest? Mmmm!"

Only half-listening and unsure who Giselle and Kate were anyway, Vanessa fiddled with the camera that was perched on her lap like a kitten. She was reclining on a long stone divan laden with enough pillows and fur throws to actually make it pretty comfortable, but hot for a July afternoon, with a nice, clear view of the pool. She watched Chuck Bass frolicking in the shallow end, clad only in a floral-print European-style bathing suit that left nothing to the imagination, while his monkey perched on the diving board, eating a bowlful of grapes.

How erotic.

She wasn't supposed to fiddle too much, so she couldn't study the shot through the viewfinder, but she was confident it was all cinematic gold: there was Chuck wading through the waist-high water, chattering into his Bluetooth headset with Sweetie chomping in the background. Behind him, Stefan, the skinny houseboy, was sweeping the flagstone path that led from the tennis courts to the main residence, trying not to accidentally whack the five overindulged pugs that were angrily attacking the broom. Every so often, she slid the camera across her lap to face Bailey Winter himself, who was wearing a vintage boy's khaki suit—short pants and all—that he'd had remade to accommodate his girth. It was the raw material for a jaw-dropping documentary.

"Don't fiddle too much, darling," clucked Bailey disapprovingly.

Vanessa smiled placidly and turned her camera back to the action in the pool. As she sat still like that, her mind drifted idly over the whirlwind of the past couple of weeks. She'd gone from Hollywood player to friendless Hamptons servant to kept woman. It was all pretty exciting, in a way, but the thing was, she missed having someone to share it with.

Vanessa surprised herself when she realized that she wasn't just staring idly into space: she was admiring Chuck Bass's perfectly toned torso, the little ripple in his muscles as he ran his fingers through his damp-but-still-perfectly-mussed dark locks. Forgetting for a minute everything she knew about the guy, every interaction she'd ever had with him, and every gross rumor she'd tried to ignore, she kind of wanted to reach out and . . . touch him. She licked her lips involuntarily.

"That's it!" Bailey Winter threw his pencil into the nearby swimming pool, then grabbed another. "You look amazing. You look satisfied and hungry all at once. Like you're ready for dessert, even though you've just had the yummiest meal ever!"

Vanessa blushed, embarrassed, and then reminded herself she wasn't admiring Chuck Bass, necessarily, just his various physical attributes. The truth was, her type was a little skinnier and paler than Chuck. The thought of Dan suddenly tugged the corners of her mouth down.

"Chin up, dear! Where's that smile gone?" Bailey Winter clapped his hands once, twice, three times, like a demented cheerleader.

Vanessa tried to will a smile onto her face, but somehow the thought of Dan had tainted everything. She missed him. And Chuck Bass's beefy chest was no substitute for love. Vanessa sighed, panning the camera around the property's emerald green lawn. Once again, all she really had was her art.

She trained the camera back on Chuck, who was now leaning up against the edge of the pool chatting with Stefan. Sweetie bobbed up and down behind him, teasing the pugs, which were barking angrily.

"Girls! Please! Quiet down!" Bailey stuck his fingers in his mouth and gave a shrill, surprisingly loud whistle. "Daddy is working! I can't concentrate with all this racket!"

"Sorry, Bailey." Chuck turned and grinned over his shoulder. "I'll try and make sure Sweetie doesn't bother them."

"What is that plague-ridden monster doing in my swimming pool anyway?" Bailey screeched, his skin turning from bronze to scarlet.

Vanessa focused her camera on the other side of the pool, and it was immediately clear to her what that plague-ridden animal was doing: Bailey's discarded pencil wasn't the only thing floating on the pool's surface.

"Tell me that is not what I think it is!" Bailey was definitely screaming now.

"I'm sorry, Bailey." Chuck waded toward the offending turd. "Sweetie can't control himself sometimes."

"Get out! Get out! I will not have you turn my sanctum sanctorum into some kind of sewer! This is East Hampton, not Calcutta!"

Vanessa pushed herself up from the divan, using both hands to steady the camera as she zoomed in quickly. This was a cinematic *gold mine*.

Yeah, or a land mine.

Air Mail - Par Avion - July 12

Dear Jenny,

I'm gay.

Love,

Dan

back in time

"We're h-o-o-o-o-o-me!" Serena's voice echoed through the foyer and deep into her parents' apartment, which she knew, as soon as she pushed the door open, was empty. It had that dark, quiet, cold quality of a home without anyone inside it, which was hardly surprising, since her parents spent more time out of the country than they did curled up on the couch. She wasn't even sure when she'd last seen them on the couch.

"God, I have to pee." Blair shoved past her and into the apartment, turning on lights as she went—the landscape of Serena's penthouse apartment was as familiar to her as that of her own home. She disappeared down the gallery hallway, making a beeline for Serena's bedroom. Nate shuffled in behind them, closing the door a little too noisily. The slam magnified in the eerily quiet rooms.

"Sorry." He shot Serena a crooked smile.

"It's okay." Serena tossed her keys onto the mahogany console table, where they landed with a clatter. "Let's find something to eat." She led Nate into the apartment and through the kitchen's swinging door.

Peering into the nearly barren Sub-Zero, Serena considered their options. "We've got some olives," she announced. "A bag of baby carrots. I think there's some cheese. You can probably find some crackers or something somewhere. I don't know where the new maid keeps everything."

It *is* so hard to find good help.

"I'll take care of it." Nate charged over to the pantry and started plundering it, removing jars and containers and setting them on the travertine counter with a bang.

"I'll load up on supplies, I guess." The whole reason they'd come back to the van der Woodsen apartment was to crash before they embarked on a road trip to find the *Charlotte*, and to stock up on the essentials: clothes and booze.

Serena made her way to the liquor cabinet that her parents had never had the foresight to lock, placing bottles of Grey Goose, Hendrick's, Havana Club, and Patrón into her Hermès tote. There was something about raiding her parents' stash while Nate and Blair puttered around her house that reminded Serena of days long past. Nothing had changed and yet everything had. That thought made her unexpectedly sad.

We all get a little moody around our birthdays.

Serena padded into her father's library and slunk into his swiveling Aeron chair. She grabbed the telephone from his desk and dialed one of the few telephone numbers she'd ever memorized.

"Hello?" Her brother Erik's voice sounded very suspicious. It was six o'clock in the morning, after all.

"It's me." Serena leaned back, placing her bare feet on her dad's old mahogany desk.

"Shit, Serena. Came up as the home number—was worried for a minute." Her brother laughed.

"They're not here." She studied the book-lined walls, examining the framed family photos of Erik playing tennis, of Serena astride a black horse, of her tanned parents sipping Campari-and-sodas at an outdoor café on the Amalfi coast. "Wimbledon," Serena and her brother said in unison.

"They're so damn predictable," Erik scoffed. "What are you doing home, anyway?"

"Just planning a little summer getaway. Thought I'd give my brother a call. And where are you exactly?"

"Connecticut," Erik told her. "I thought Dad might be calling to say they were coming out."

Serena glanced through the French doors into the living room, where Nate was chasing Blair around a buttoned-leather ottoman, trying to stick cornichons in her ears. "We're taking a road trip," Serena told him. "You want to come? We've got room in the car for one more."

And maybe she didn't feel like being the third wheel?

"Tempting. But I'm kind of digging it up here. How about a pit stop in Ridgefield instead?"

She did some quick mental planning—they could crash here today, then head out tomorrow morning. Then maybe she could convince Blair and Nate to spend a night in Ridgefield, and hopefully someone would realize that the next day was her birthday. "I think we can arrange that."

Serena said goodbye to her brother, replacing the phone on her dad's desk. She glanced toward the closet, wondering idly if her parents had stashed a surprise birthday present for her somewhere in the apartment.

Aren't surprises always the most fun?

Blair yawned—the kind of deep yawn you feel all through your body—and ran Serena's Mason Pearson brush through her hair roughly. She'd never been one of those one-thousand-strokes-of-the-brush-before-bed types but still, it couldn't hurt. It was only eight o'clock in the morning and the sun was streaming in through the window, but it seemed like years, not hours, since she'd had a proper night's sleep.

"I can't believe I'm so tired." Serena collapsed onto the wide plain of her bed, arms and legs stretched out around her.

"Yeah." Nate hesitated at the foot of the bed, glancing at Blair, who was standing by the mirror, and then down at Serena, lying prone in front of him.

"I'm done." Serena unbuttoned her jeans and wiggled out of them without standing up. "I can't even get under the blankets."

Blair glanced at Serena's long, tapered legs and then at Nate looking at those same legs. She felt a familiar pang of jealousy inside her chest. She'd loved and been jealous of Serena for as long as she'd known her, which was pretty much forever. But things were finally different. The year had been filled with so many ups and downs, but it was finally summer, they were going to Yale together in the fall, and they had the rest of their lives as best friends ahead of them. And she had Nate, right here, right now, right in front of her.

Now who's forgetting about someone?

Blair slipped her borrowed pale pink Lacoste polo over her head and then reached up her back to unclasp her bra, which she let fall to the ground casually. "Nate, can I sleep in your shirt?" she asked shyly.

"Course." Nate nodded eagerly, trying to look away. He pulled his cotton tee off and tossed it to her.

She pulled it over her head, pausing inside the darkness of it to breathe in his overwhelming scent: his armpits and his laundry detergent, a hint of pot smoke and toothpaste.

Good enough to eat.

By the time she popped her head through the head hole in the still-warm T-shirt, Nate had kicked off his khakis and crashed out on the bed next to Serena in a pair of funny palm-tree-printed boxer shorts that Blair was pretty sure had been a present from her.

She switched off the bedroom's overhead light. The morning summer sun was pouring through the bedroom window, illuminating the bodies of her friends. She walked over to the foot of the bed, then carefully wedged herself between Serena, who was already sleeping, her breaths long and muted, like a baby's, and an almost-naked Nate.

"'Night," Nate whispered.

"'Night," she quietly repeated. Her heart pounding in her ears, Blair suddenly felt wide awake. She studied the delicately molded and crenellated panels of Serena's ceiling as she listened to the light snore of her best friend and tried to ignore the soft skin of her other best friend—the only guy she had ever really loved—whose arm was grazing hers ever so slightly. How was she *ever* going to fall asleep?

Then she felt fingers trailing down her arm, so delicately it tickled. Nate's hand slid down over her wrist, then slipped into her palm, giving it a gentle squeeze.

Letting out a sigh, it felt like she was breathing out

something she didn't even know was inside of her. The frustration, the jealousy, the worry over what would happen next. She turned to look at him, but his eyes were closed, and soon hers were too. And that's how they slept, for the rest of the day and into the night.

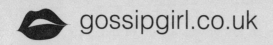
hey people!

You know who I've always felt kind of sorry for? Those kids with summer birthdays. They never got to have ice cream parties at Serendipity because all their friends were away at camp or whiling away the season in Amagansett. They never got to bring pastel-buttercream-frosted Magnolia cupcakes for the whole class to enjoy. They never got to have the coveted tea party at the Plaza with all their best girlfriends. All because they just happened to be born during the three months of the year when the last thing anyone wants to think about is anyone but themselves. We don't *mean* to be so selfish, it's just . . . in the air. But that doesn't mean we don't feel bad about it. Really. So this one's for you, birthday girls . . .

Top three ways to say, *I'm so sorry I missed your birthday while I was making out with my unbelievably hot summer fling:*

1) Take her to Barneys and let her use your credit card for as many minutes as she is old. When your mom gets the bill, take the rap, because that's what friends are for.

2) Apologize for being more interested in your summer romance than in her rite of passage, and invite her to join you and your new beau on a double date with his slightly cross-eyed but almost-as-cute younger brother.

3) It's summer, remember, so full-body maintenance is more important than usual. Splurge on a full-on Bliss spa experience (not just some lame gift-from-great-aunt-Susie mani-pedi combo, please) so your best pal can be as tanned, hairless, and pampered as you already are.

your e-mail

Dear GG,
I'm worried that I might be turning gay. Do you know if there are warning signs?
—Blue Boy

Dear BB,
Warning signs aplenty:
1) You refer to things as "fabulous" or "genius" and have used the word *swish* in the last twenty-four hours.
2) Your best friend is a heavy girl with an interest in the theater.
3) Your ringtone is a Gwen Stefani song.
4) When the weather turns warm, you'd rather watch the shirt-less skater boys than the topless sunbathers in Sheep Meadow.
5) You write to a wise authority because you want her to break the news you already know but just can't admit: you're gay. It's okay!

Love life. Love boys. Love yourself.
—GG

Q: Dear GG,

Not actually a letter so much as an announcement: I'm planning a big blowout at my country place in celebration of my little sister's eighteenth. So if you're going to be in Connecticut or are down for a road trip, make sure you look up your old friends who summer in that great state. If I'm one of them, you're totally on the guest list.

—Pool Party in Connecticut

A: Dear PP in C,

Connecticut's a bit outside my usual party radius, but I suppose getting there is half the fun—after all, the road trip is a great American tradition. The wind in your hair, the hot sun on the pavement, the freedom of going whichever direction you choose—sentiments most memorably captured by Jack Kerouac in *On the Road*. Although honestly, all I remember from that book was lots of drugs and lots of randomness. Talk about following the yellow brick road! But if your "blowout" is as big as promised, I'm psyched to see your Emerald City. Did that sound as dirty as I think it did? Oops. Anyway, consider the party announced!

—GG

Q: Dear GG,

I'm totally miserable because my parents say I have to get a job this summer. But then I was thinking about it, and I realized working doesn't have to suck—*you* have the coolest job ever! So I was wondering, do you take interns?

—Please Hire Me!

Dear PHM,

Thanks for the flattery, and trust me, you're not wrong—this *is* the coolest job in the world. Although the truth is, I really don't think of it as a job, but rather as a public service. Sort of like being a superhero: Bat Girl, Super Girl, Gossip Girl . . . You get the picture. Sadly, though, there's only room for one Gossip Girl at this iBook. Good luck finding an internship elsewhere! I hear *Vogue* is hiring custodial specialists . . . Just kidding.
—GG

bills, bills, bills

That last e-mail got me thinking about how for an unfortunate few of you, the term "summer job" is not just a phenomenon seen in the movies but a day-to-day reality. My heart goes out to you, seriously. But it's not *all* bad. Here are some positive points to bear in mind when you're punching the time clock:

1) The best way to meet people is at work, whether it's a cute coworker or a cute customer. (Anybody remember how **D** first came across yoga girl? Let me tell you, it wasn't by wandering into a Bikram class . . .)

2) What better way to learn the value of a hard day's work and feel the satisfaction of earning your money? Ha! Are they still telling those lies?

3) I hear hard labor burns a ton of calories!

So to PHM, keep your chin up, and keep on plugging! That's all for now, dears. This little worker bee needs to refresh her makeup, recharge her laptop battery, and pack up for a little road trip . . .

You know you love me.

gossip girl

d, hot and bothered again

"Davey, Humphrey, Bogart, whatever your name is, speed it up."

All the managers at the Strand had the same authoritative bark that never failed to make Dan stand up a little straighter. He looked left and right but couldn't tell where the command had come from.

"You waiting for an engraved invitation, madam?" Phil, a balding, failed Ph.D. candidate who loved to make the afternoon shifts hell, popped his head around an old rusty metal shelf.

"Asshole," Dan muttered as he pushed the groaning cart of to-be-shelved books.

Sensitive much?

The cracked rubber wheels squeaked and clacked as Dan pushed the rickety cart down the long, narrow aisle, past the outdated travel guides. He took a deep breath, immersing himself in the familiar rhythm of picking up a book, determining the last name of the author, and locating its spot on the shelf. It was a sure way to let his subconscious speak to him:

Hairy kiss—burn my chin
The sick taste of absinthe in my throat
Deep in my gullet; sore lips and
Punches in the gut
Blind corners turned and now I am nowhere . . .

His poetic free association was interrupted when an over-size book slipped off his cart. He bent over to pick it up, reading the title: *Everything You've Always Wanted to Know (Go Ahead, Admit It!) About Gay Sex* by Melvin Lloyd and Dr. Stephen Furman.

The line drawing on the glossy cover showed two male forms embracing chastely. Like brothers. Or baseball players after a game. Totally normal. Glancing around to see if any-one was near—as usual, no one was interested in the travel guides to New Zealand published in the 1970s—Dan opened the book, whistling all casual-like.

Nice try.

The slick pages slipped through his fingers, revealing more line drawings of two muscular fellows in various embraces, arms and tongues positioned here and there. There were a number of bullet points and lists of dos and don'ts. He skimmed the book, heart pounding, taking in only snatches of phrases like "Insert your tongue" and "Some partners find the use of an elbow helpful" and "Remember to brush your teeth."

Pausing again to make sure that he was alone, Dan skipped ahead to the back of the book, where the heavier paper stock meant only one thing: photographs. And there they were, in full-color glory: two men, performing what at first glance looked like a gymnastic routine.

Dan's throat suddenly felt very dry. He slammed the book shut and stuffed it on the very bottom of his pile. He'd never needed a cigarette this badly in his life.

Breathe, breathe.

Shaking slightly, Dan inhaled deeply on a beloved Camel and stepped away from the Strand. He needed a walk to purge his mind of the mental images of those two thick-necked wrestler types in unimaginable poses. Not that he had any kind of problem with gay people, of course. *They're here, they're queer, it's awesome.* But there were some things that people just weren't meant to do with their bodies. Like running. And yoga. And . . . whatever it was you called the thing he had just seen depicted in that book.

Yoga. He'd had a brush with that stuff—that was the closest he'd come to contorting his body into a shape resembling what the guys in the book were doing, and he was not eager to get into that particular position again anytime soon. The only reason he'd bothered with yoga in the first place had been for a girl. He'd been so crazed over Bree he'd experimented with all kinds of insane things: yoga, running, organic fruit juice. Maybe the same thing was happening with Greg? He'd never really met anyone who loved books as much as he did. Maybe he was just getting everything all mixed up? Maybe it was just like his dad had said and he was just transferring his passion for books onto their friendship?

Yup—like quasi-gay father, like quasi-gay son.

Dodging the summer tourist sidewalk traffic, Dan stubbed out his cigarette and stuffed his hands deep into the pockets of his fraying brown cords. *You can't be gay.* The image of Bree naked and glistening with sweat in that overheated yoga studio came to him, and suddenly he felt a little out of breath. A little dizzy. What was this sensation? It felt familiar and alien all at once. And he felt something else too— a boner. In full daylight, like a little kid. Looking down at it, he couldn't help but smile. It was the best boner he'd ever had! The thought of Bree, her bare skin damp with sweat as she arched her back and planted her palms on the floor, was what sent his heart racing.

He lit another cigarette to celebrate the fact that he had biological evidence to prove that he, Dan Humphrey, was most certainly not gay. He had to keep himself from jumping in the air to click his heels together.

Oh, and *that's* not gay at all.

the ghost of high school past

"Girls! There are girls here!" yelled a guy Serena didn't recognize. He lurched down the stone steps from the foyer to the driveway, clutching one of her mother's antique crystal champagne flutes. He raised the glass in salute as she stepped out of the Aston Martin, sloshing champagne all over the stone steps.

"Dude, that's my sister." Erik van der Woodsen pushed the staggering guy out of his way and raced toward Serena. He wore a rumpled blue gingham oxford, top three buttons undone, and khakis that had started to fray at the cuffs. His pale blond hair was mussed and his huge blue eyes were bloodshot, but he was as handsome as ever. "Howdy, sis."

"Got the party started, I see." Serena hugged her brother excitedly. "In case you forgot, my birthday's not till tomorrow."

"You only turn eighteen once." He threw his arms around her and lifted her off her feet easily. "Happy almost birthday."

"This is for me?" Serena asked, a smile spreading across her face. Okay, so it wasn't *exactly* her idea of a birthday party, but it was sweet that her brother had remembered.

Even if it was probably just a convenient excuse for a blowout.

Probably?

Behind her, Blair and Nate shuffled out of the backseat. Serena had volunteered to drive since she knew how to get here the best, and Blair could only drive automatics, but did they really have to ride in the backseat together *again?* What was she, the chauffeur?

Kind of looks that way.

"What's up, guys?" Erik greeted them.

"Hey." Nate nodded at Erik. "Good call on the party. I almost forgot that tomorrow's your birthday," he said, turning to Serena.

Blair slipped her hand into her best friend's. "What's an appropriate afternoon cocktail, birthday girl?"

Is there one that's *not* appropriate?

The scene by the pool was like something out of a screwball college comedy. A gaggle of obviously drunk guys in board shorts cannonballed into the water, splashing their buddies seated nearby. A crowd lingered near the double-height French doors that led to the library—and the well-stocked bar. And there were so few girls in evidence—a couple stretched out on chaises near the diving board and a trio of giggling girls attempting some kind of drinking game—that wherever they congregated, a drooling group of boys was not far off. Someone had rigged an iPod to the van der Woodsens' stereo system, and the insistent thrum of the new Arctic Monkeys album filled the air.

"This is finally starting to feel like summer vacation." Blair slipped her feet out of her white leather Prada flip-flops and propped them on the edge of the wrought-iron garden table. She swirled the ice in her Bloody Mary distractedly.

"Something like that." Serena leaned back in the uncomfortable chair and scanned the crowd that had gathered, supposedly, for her birthday celebration. The guys outnumbered the girls by a ratio of about ten million to one, and though she recognized some of them—Erik's old tennis teammates, his roommate at Brown—she didn't see many familiar faces in the crowd. She might be the birthday girl, but she wondered if anyone even knew who she was.

It's her party and she'll pout if she wants to.

"Shit." Blair tilted her head back and drained her glass. "I guess I was thirsty. You want another?"

Serena shook her head, almost spilling her untouched Cosmopolitan. "I'm good."

"I'll be right back."

Serena watched from behind her enameled Selima aviators as Blair launched out of her seat and padded toward the bar. Erik was presiding over the bottles of booze lined up like toy soldiers on the elaborate carved mahogany bar. Nate was lingering on the fringes of the crowd, his hands shoved deep in the pockets of his tattered khaki shorts. Serena watched as he pretended not to see Blair skipping through the crowd toward him.

Interesting.

She'd woken up this morning to the sound of Blair's giggles, but when she'd asked what was funny, Blair had sighed and said, "Just Natie." *Natie?* Then, in the car, she kept glancing back at them in the rearview mirror, but every time Blair was just staring placidly out the window, and Nate was resting his eyes. Nothing amiss. So why did she feel so . . . weird?

She raised her glass and swallowed a small sip of the tart cocktail, finally recognizing someone in the crowd: a broad-chested, curly-brown-haired guy was seated at the edge of the pool, legs dangling in the water. His brown eyes had a familiar sparkle as he took in the scene around him, drumming his long, tapered fingers on the neck of his beer bottle. The tiniest suggestion of a grin played on his full lips, and Serena knew that behind those lips were two rows of brilliant white teeth. She could picture his smile, she could practically hear the tremulous sound of his voice as he whispered the words she'd run away from. That was the last time she'd seen him, exactly one year ago.

Henry was the bassist in Hanover's jazz band. He was tall and cute with dark curls that fell into his eyes, and a mischievous smile. Serena's dorm room had been right under his, and late at night she'd throw her textbooks at the ceiling, waiting for him to drop something loud and heavy on the floor in response. Sometimes—actually, a lot—they'd hang out on the roof and drink whiskey and smoke cigars. They'd been good friends, and then the year had ended and they'd wound up in Ridgefield together—his family lived there year round, and she summered there. The night before her seventeenth birthday she and Henry had stayed up late, drinking and talking, and had wound up on their backs on the tennis court, waiting for shooting stars, and eventually kissing. Then, Henry said it: "I love you." Instead of saying it back, Serena fled into the house, booked a plane to Paris to join her brother, Erik, in his travels, and never spoke to Henry again. It wasn't that she didn't like him. Honestly, she did. But love was unmistakable, and at that time, there was only one boy she could ever truly love. Then, and maybe now, too . . .

Serena tipped her glass back and gulped its contents, her hands shaking. *Leave it to me to have a nervous breakdown the night before my eighteenth birthday,* she thought.

"Hey. Remember me?"

Henry's voice gave her a little start. "I was wondering when you were going to come over and say hello." She pulled her knees up to her chest and smiled at him.

"I could say the same thing." The chair's legs scraped noisily on the concrete as he pulled it out and took a seat. "You look great."

"Thank you." She smiled shyly, taking a sip of her drink. She fumbled nervously for her cigarettes, which were lying on the table near the trunk of the big umbrella.

Henry lit her shaking Gauloise and then helped himself to one from her stash. Serena exhaled a long plume of smoke, which danced away in the breeze.

"What happened to you, anyway?" Henry smiled thoughtfully, studying Serena's face. "I mean . . . you just *left.*"

Serena looked away.

"I e-mailed you a few times," Henry continued. "I never heard back from you . . . And when I tried again, your school account had been closed."

"I guess I needed to be alone for a little while to sort some things out. And then I went back to the city." She pulled a strand of hair out from behind her ear and played with it distractedly, smiling sadly. "It's a long story." One even she didn't understand, and one she'd never told anyone.

Is that a fact?

Serena stared over Henry's shoulder at the crowd of rev-elers: some of them half-naked and soaking up the sun, others dancing at speeds not altogether appropriate to the music. And then there was Blair, sipping yet another Bloody Mary and smiling up shyly at Nate, who gripped a beer, grinning stupidly. Serena glanced back at Henry. It was like a time warp: Blair and Nate completely oblivious to her, and Henry staring devotedly at her from the other side of the table like nothing had changed.

"This is my birthday party, you know," she said at last.

"You think I don't know that?" Henry reached over and grasped her hand with his slightly callused musician's fingers. "That's why I came. It's our anniversary." Serena swallowed.

Happy birthday!

behind the scenes

"We're inside the aviary now." Vanessa was practically shouting to be heard over the chirps and cries of the brightly colored birds that were frantically swirling around the glass-enclosed room. Vanessa held her camera steadily and spun around to get a complete 360-degree look at the massive, plant-filled room. Birds of every hue, from egg yolk yellow to Tiffany blue to Bloody Mary scarlet, fluttered around on clipped wings, drifting from bough to bough in a pathetic attempt at the flight they'd never again experience.

"I'm told that this is where Bailey Winter does most of his preliminary sketches," Vanessa continued. "In fact, those who know his work well may recognize the colors from his most recent couture collection." She trained the camera on a little bird chirping in the branches of a potted banana plant.

The shot looked so alive—the colorful birds spinning and flitting all around the high-ceilinged aviary, the sun spilling down in fat beams of light. The composition was flawless, symmetrical but still dynamic. She started mentally planning a whole series of documentaries on the creative processes of different artists. Maybe she'd do one on Dan and really capture the writer's life. And one on Ken Mogul, to explore what it was like to be a world-famous filmmaker.

And a weirdo.

The glass-topped rattan table was scattered with sheets of scribbled-on paper, pencils, and half-drained martini glasses. Vanessa made her way over to the workstation and focused the shot on some unfinished sketches.

"A few months from now these pencil sketches will have been transformed into chiffon and silk." Vanessa was trying her hardest to remember the names of fabrics she'd heard Blair mention during their short stint as roommates. "Just think of it: right now these ideas are merely doodles, but soon they may be walking down the red carpet at the Oscars."

Vanessa adjusted the focus to capture the faint line drawings more clearly.

"And so we see now even more clearly how the designer Bailey Winter's creative process works. It begins with something as simple as the color of plumage. After some pencil sketches and a few martinis . . ." She trailed off, because really, she had no idea how to describe dresses or fashion or if chiffon was really the name of a fabric. Maybe it was a dessert? "The only thing I cannot show you is that which exists only inside the designer's mind. That's the true creative process." *Or the true drunken process.* She turned the camera on the army of not-quite-empty wineglasses.

"Oh. My. God."

Vanessa whirled around, instinctively hiding the camera behind her back as she did.

Oops.

"*What* are you doing in here?" Bailey slammed the glass door behind him to keep any of his precious birds from escaping into the garden. "Vanessa, Vanessa," he clucked, sounding exactly like a chicken. "The aviary is strictly off-limits. This is where I come to think and be inspired! You'll disturb the balance of creative energy simply by being in here!"

Of course! The energy balance!

"Please, dear, just back away a little. Not the drawings. No one can see them until I'm done with the preliminary sketches."

"Sorry." Vanessa lamely backed away, trying to look repentant. An aquamarine-speckled parakeet squawked past her ear violently. "I guess I was just making myself at home. You know, like you'd suggested."

"Well, there's being a good guest and then there's just plain intruding." Bailey frowned, hugging his papers to his chest and shielding them from Vanessa's view. "You may go anywhere in the compound you like *except* for the aviary. This is my sacred space, dear. I'm spiritually naked when I step past those doors."

Well, as long as he *literally* keeps his clothes on . . .

"I'll be more careful in the future," Vanessa promised him, backing away slowly, still keeping the camera out of sight behind her back.

"Yes, yes, I know you will," Bailey replied, placing his papers back on the desk, but shielding them with his chubby, outstretched arms. "All is forgiven."

"Okay, well, I'll just be going then." Vanessa turned quickly and started to bolt from the room.

"Eeeeeeek!" Bailey's screech drove the birds into a frenzy.

Suddenly, hundreds of scared starlings dashed for safety, darting up toward the ceiling as far as their crippled wings would take them.

"Yes?" Vanessa asked, still lamely trying to hide the camera with her hands.

"I-I-Is that a . . . *camera*?"

Brilliant observation.

"Bailey, let me explain." Vanessa felt her face flush. "I was just hoping, I mean, I was only interested in, I needed to, you know, I wanted to document the creative process, like the ideas behind, and what goes into, I mean, the whole story of—"

Bailey leapt out of his seat and stood, trembling, staring at Vanessa. "Just tell me. I need to know . . . Did you? You didn't. I mean, you didn't *film* in here, did you?"

"Uh, no?"

Nice save.

"These sketches are top secret! Oh my dear. My goodness me. Do you know what would happen if they got out? Do you know that there are people who would pay . . . well, I don't know what, but they would pay dearly for a glimpse, for just a *hint* of what I have planned for the coming seasons. I simply can't risk the competition." He looked like he was about to faint. "Oh my . . ."

"Bailey, I promise you, I wasn't going to sell your secrets or anything like that. I'm just a filmmaker, you know, and I thought this would be a great subject for a documentary." Vanessa smiled at him hopefully. A lime-colored macaw landed on his shoulder, and he batted it away. "Maybe I should go . . ." Vanessa suggested, suddenly concerned that Bailey would demand she turn over all the film she'd shot over the past couple of days.

"Yes, off to your room." Bailey looked like he was on the verge of tears. "I need a moment to collect my thoughts. We'll discuss what's to be done about your misbehavior at dinner."

"Right." Vanessa frowned. Was he *really* sending her to her room? That hadn't happened to her . . . well, ever. No one had ever sent Vanessa Abrams to her room! She'd go to her room all right; she'd go to her room and pack. Documentary or no, she'd had about enough of the Hamptons and Bailey's absurdities to last her a lifetime. As for dinner, well, if all went well, by that time she'd be safely on a train headed back to the city and the only place she really felt at home anymore: Dan Humphrey's apartment.

Home is where the heart is!

those three little words

"How about a refill?"

Blair shook her head and pointed at her ears to indicate that she couldn't really hear Nate over the roar of the party, which had gotten considerably livelier as the day wound down. The afternoon sun was still high overhead, but the revelers were hot and hungry and drunk. Erik had thoughtfully ignited the enormous gas grill and dispatched those guests still sober enough to drive to the grocery store. That distinctly summertime smell of barbecue wafted through the air, giving Blair a head rush.

Or maybe it was the four Bloody Marys.

Nate leaned down and whispered in her ear. "I said, I'm going in for a refill. You want something?"

His hot breath tickled her neck, and she closed her eyes to keep the room steady. "I'll take a glass of water."

"Easy." Nate took her arm, led her into the library, and sat her down on the worn brown suede sofa before heading into the kitchen for a drink.

Blair yawned. Long car rides always made her sleepy,

and last night hadn't exactly been restful, even if they had basically slept for twenty-four hours. How could she sleep with Nate breathing right next to her all night? Every time she'd wanted to turn over or rearrange her pillows, she just couldn't, not if it meant letting go of Nate's hand. She closed her eyes thinking about it.

"Hey there, sleeping beauty." Blair felt a pair of soft lips graze her forehead. She smiled, keeping her eyes shut tight. It felt like forever since she'd felt those lips on her face. But when she finally let her heavy lids flutter open she gasped. The lips belonged not to Nate, but to Erik van der Woodsen. His grinning face loomed over her. A handsome prince, but not the *right* handsome prince.

Too many princes, too little time . . .

"Hey Erik." Blair grabbed a nearby throw cushion and hugged it to her chest. He looked just like Serena, except a boy. From his blond hair to his casual, all-is-right-with-the-world stride, to the way he held his broad, tennis-toned shoulders, to the funny little wrinkle that formed at the corners of his almost–navy blue eyes when he smiled. It seemed like a million years ago when they'd sort of had a thing.

Been there, done that.

"Scoot over." Erik plopped down next to her, draping his arm along the back of the couch. He sighed deeply. "This party is so out of hand I haven't even had a chance to talk to anyone."

"That's the sign of a good party," Blair observed sleepily. She peeked out the open door, looking for Nate, but he'd been swallowed up by all the partygoers waiting for refills at the bar.

"Dude, I mean, I haven't even seen you since, what, was it that time in Sun Valley?" Blair noticed that his words were starting to run together. He was even more wasted than she was.

"I guess," Blair responded distractedly, even though they'd seen each other in passing at her and Serena's Constance Billard graduation only a few weeks prior. It didn't seem worth bringing up right now—in fact, all she could think about was getting out of this conversation, not prolonging it.

My, how times have changed.

"You look so beautiful." He stroked Blair's hair with his tanned hand and grinned at her drunkenly and a little suggestively.

"Here's your water." Nate appeared seemingly out of nowhere, proffering an ice-cold bottle of Pellegrino.

Blair sat up a little straighter. Her knight in shining armor. Or faded khaki.

"'Sup, Nate?" Erik slurred, leaning against Blair. "You having a good time?"

"Yeah, totally," Nate agreed. "But I think everyone's getting kind of hungry. Those guys just got back from the store but they can't figure out how to turn up the grill."

"I'm the grill master, man." Erik stood and yawned, stretching his arms out wide. "Blair, find me later?" He clapped Nate on the shoulder and then disappeared out the door and into the crowd.

"Thanks for that." Blair sipped greedily at the cold water.

Nate grinned. "He's wasted. It looked like you needed saving."

Will you always be the one to save me? She almost said it out loud as she thought it. It was a line from *Breakfast at Fred's*. She'd run lines with Serena so many times that she'd committed the entire script to memory. In the movie that was her life, Nate was the gorgeous leading man who would always be there to swoop in and rescue her.

Nate settled onto the couch—still warm from the weight of Erik's body—and dug into his pockets for his lighter, which he flicked idly. He narrowed his gold-flecked green eyes in concentration; a gesture Blair knew meant he was either deep in thought or spaced out in a marijuana-induced haze. Finally, he looked up, meeting her gaze. Blair was surprised to feel her breath catch in her throat.

"Do you think maybe we could go upstairs . . . and . . ." He trailed off.

"Upstairs?" She took a gulp of water. She'd been with Nate a million times, talked to him a million times, kissed him a million times. There was nothing new here, yet something felt completely different.

"Yeah," he muttered, flicking his lighter nervously. "I thought maybe we could go upstairs and . . . talk?"

"Talk," she repeated. The song changed from something by Clap Your Hands Say Yeah to "Hey Ya." Even though the song was totally old, the floor started to shake with everybody dancing outside and in the van der Woodsens' living room.

"I just . . ." he started, flicking his lighter again. "I—"

Blair suddenly stood and grabbed Nate's hand, pulling him off of the couch. She wanted to listen to whatever it was that he was trying so seriously to say, and she wanted to be able to hear it. She pulled Nate out of the library and through the crowded living room, holding his hand so she wouldn't lose him in the crowd. Blair slipped by Serena at the bottom of the stairs without saying anything to her. She of all people would understand. Blair was halfway up the wide, polished mahogany staircase when she felt Nate stop behind her.

"What's wrong?" she asked, turning around.

"I . . . I . . . have to tell you something," Nate stammered.

"Upstairs," she urged, pulling on his arm. He didn't budge, so she turned around again, looking down at him from the step above. They were almost the same height.

"It's just that . . ." Nate stuttered. Then he looked up and met her gaze. "I love you," he finally whispered.

At last.

wait till the midnight hour

"I love you."

The voice was unmistakably Nate's and the words were clear as day to her even over the cries of a gyrating hippie townie chick flailing her arms to "Hey Ya" as she smacked Serena in the face with her long, essential-oil-scented dreadlocks.

He loved Blair.

Serena never would have guessed Nate Archibald was so in touch with his emotions, but she knew it was true—he did love Blair. She'd seen the meaningful looks Nate and Blair had been trading ever since their daring breakout from Bailey Winter's compound. And then yesterday, the way Blair had wedged her way in between them when they went to bed had been so *obvious*. Serena felt a sinking feeling in her stomach, like when the road falls out from underneath the car more quickly than you're prepared for: it was *her* birthday—almost, anyway—and it was *her* party—technically, anyway. She was the one who deserved a little love and affection, wasn't she?

She hesitated. Perched between the delicately wall-papered

wall and a massive grandfather clock, she had the perfect cover to do a little observing.

Like, spying?

She peered out around the clock and up at Nate and Blair on the stairs, making wordless and intense eye contact. Then Blair twined her fingers through Nate's and the two of them disappeared up the stairs, taking a left at the landing. They were heading to her parents' master suite. Serena closed her eyes, fighting her way through the crowd to the bar. There was always whiskey, and Henry, and cigars. Not necessarily in that order.

"There you are." Serena stumbled a little but kept a tight grip on the crystal tumbler she'd filled—again—from the bottle of her father's Oban whiskey she'd hid from the rest of the revelers. It was her birthday and her house—why not save the good stuff for herself?

"Serena." Henry's familiar voice split the night. It felt like a hug just knowing he was nearby. He was so handsome, and he probably still loved her . . .

And maybe she was just a *little* drunk?

Someone had managed to get the van der Woodsens' back garden fire pit going, and Henry and three guys Serena didn't recognize were huddled around it, warming themselves against the surprisingly brisk summer evening. Except for the flickering flames and the stars high overhead, the night was dark. It was a comforting, familiar kind of darkness. Serena had spent so many summer nights here, like the night she ditched Henry.

"I've been looking for you." Serena settled down next to

him on one of the low stone benches that encircled the fire pit. She was wearing an ancient pair of Seven cutoffs and he was still in his swim trunks. Their bare knees were almost touching.

"Well, you found me." He used the tiny stub of the cigarette he was smoking to ignite a new one.

"This is your birthday party, right?" asked one of the other guys, who Serena recognized as one of her brother's Brown freshman year suitemates, although she couldn't remember his name.

"It's my birthday tomorrow." Serena glanced at her slim Chanel watch. "In approximately ninety-seven minutes, actually. And it's also Bastille Day."

"*Vive la France.*" Henry raised the bottle of Corzo tequila in his hands and clinked it against her glass.

"*Vive la France.*" Serena tipped her glass back, draining her whiskey in one gulp. "I missed you," she added, even though it was sort of untrue. As soon as she'd returned to the city, she'd forgotten all about Henry.

"I missed you too." Henry popped the bottle open and refilled her glass and then his, then passed the bottle to his left. "Let's have our own little prebirthday celebration."

Serena looked up at the glittering stars overhead. Everything around her was bringing her back to a year ago, and then two years ago, when everything had been so different but also exactly the same. She turned her head, meeting Henry's gaze. She wanted to let him distract her all over again. She needed him to distract her so she could try and forget about what was probably happening right now on her parents' bed.

"And what happens at midnight?" she asked, sniffing the tequila tentatively.

"At midnight?" Henry clinked his glass against hers and tossed the shot back down his throat. "That's when you get your present."

If she can stay awake that long.

love is in the air

"You boys okay in there?" Rufus Humphrey poked his crazy-haired head into the living room. "I can't get you anything else? I've got some almond-and-lentil pesto in the blender."

"No, Mr. Humphrey, you've been too kind already!" Greg smiled graciously and turned to Dan. "Your dad's a riot."

Dan took a deep breath and used the remote control to crank the volume on the Humphreys' battered old television, which was tuned to a documentary on the Beats. Though he had no memory of it, he'd apparently extended a drunken invitation to Greg to watch it together.

Who knows what else he offered up in his drunken state?

"Um." Dan thoughtlessly shoveled popcorn into his mouth, eager to have something to do with his hands. "Thanks for bringing this."

"No problem." Greg reached into the plastic bowl, his fingers brushing against Dan's as he grabbed a handful. "You mentioned that your dad isn't much of a cook, so I thought I should come prepared."

I did? "Yeah, well, it's a good thing." Dan chuckled nervously, noticing now that his dad had displayed the freaky penis vase on a book-laden shelf. The paint on the crumbly living room was looking particularly water-stained.

"*In vino veritas.*" Greg giggled.

Dan recognized the Latin phrase suggesting that people are more likely to say what they really feel when drunk. *In wine there is truth.* His dad said it all the time before downing a whole bottle of Merlot.

"Dude, look at Kerouac. He's so . . . electric," Greg observed.

Dan studied the famous writers on the flickering screen. He was electric, wasn't he? He was almost . . . handsome. Was it totally gay to think that? Dan felt his stomach lurch. There was something uncomfortably familiar about this scene: sitting on the couch, the warmth and weight of another body next to his, a cerebral documentary on the screen. What did this remind him of?

What? Or *who*?

Dan might have been totally clueless, but he knew what was coming next: the lights were turned down low, the television was alive with stories of rollicking, devil-may-care outlaw writers, the evening was warm, the couch was cozy: there was only one way this could end, and that was with a make-out session.

Another make-out session, to be more specific.

"I can't see very well. Can you?" Dan reached to his left and switched on the chipped ceramic table lamp, helping to break the room's romantic mood a little.

"Now I can see you better." Greg smiled coyly at Dan.

"Right." Dan took the oversize plastic bowl off of his lap and wedged it into the small space between him and Greg. "That should give you easier access," he explained.

Dan patted at his pockets anxiously. He was dying for a cigarette . . . but did he dare risk it? Dan was pretty sure there was nothing sexier than smoking: the little burst of flame as you struck the match, the languorous exhale of long plumes of smoke. He didn't want to send Greg the wrong message.

Yeah, we all love smoker's breath. Not.

There were a few minutes of silence, during which Dan tried to focus on the television but couldn't stop monitoring Greg's every movement in his peripheral vision. Greg kept running his hand over his soft blond crew cut and chewing on his slightly chapped bottom lip.

"You don't like the movie?" Greg caught Dan's eye. He reached for the remote control and turned the volume down enough to make the television nothing more than ambient background noise.

"No, no, it's not that," Dan stammered. "I was just . . . thinking about what we should do at our next salon meeting."

"I think we should do the Beats." Greg pulled his feet up onto the couch and rested his chin on his knees. He had a layer of soft-looking blond stubble on his face. We could even screen this documentary . . . I mean, if you want to."

Dan looked at the black-and-white footage of a couple of shirtless poets drinking bottles of beer and smoking cigarettes. He nodded miserably. There was no use fighting fate, was there? He was gay now—everywhere he turned there were signs from the universe telling him to just go with it. So why couldn't he just put his arm around Greg's shoulders and nuzzle into his neck? It didn't seem wrong, but it didn't seem quite right, either.

"Kerouac! Christ, it just doesn't get any better, does it?" Apparently, Rufus Humphrey had entered the room unobserved. He was standing behind the couch, breathing over their heads.

Thank goodness for nosy dads.

Rufus leaned in to murmur in Dan's ear. "It was a different time, I tell you. We didn't have any regard for rules or the rigid definitions of society. We all just . . . were. You know what I mean?"

"Sounds amazing," Greg agreed, leaning in closer to Dan. He smelled like popcorn and laundry detergent. He smelled delicious. In a nongay way.

"Dad! Join us!" Dan jerked away, grabbing onto the sofa's arm as though it were a life preserver. He grabbed the bowl of popcorn and patted the empty space on the couch. "Plenty of room for one more!"

"Really?" Rufus exclaimed. Then, in a surprisingly graceful move for such a massive man, he leapt over the back of the couch and landed squarely between the two boys. "Don't mind if I do!"

Dan exhaled. He'd never been so happy to see his dad before. "Yeah, watch with us. And maybe after you can tell us all your stories about the good old days?"

Rufus studied his son suspiciously. His neon green tank top was pulled tight over his belly and tucked into a pair of Dan's navy blue school gym shorts. "You want to hear my old stories?"

"Definitely." Dan nodded excitedly. "I'm sure Greg does too!"

"Sure." Greg nodded politely.

"Yes, tell us *everything*." Dan smiled. His dad's stories were always endless and nonsensical. And totally unromantic.

let's get it on

"So." Blair exhaled sexily, her voice husky and low. She'd lost count of how many cocktails she'd had, but she felt completely sober now. *I love you. I love you.* He loved her. She leaned back on the pale yellow Frette pillows on the bed in the van der Woodsens' quiet master suite. The pumping music downstairs and the sounds of drunken revelers outside were hushed by the gentle hum of the A/C.

"So." Nate stood at the foot of the bed, grinning at her excitedly. His cheeks were flushed and his green eyes gleamed. He shifted his weight from foot to foot, looking more like he was waiting in line for the bathroom than waiting to pounce on her.

Blair patted the soft feather duvet beside her. "Get over here," she said with a knowing smile.

Yes, ma'am.

Nate kicked off his gray-blue canvas deck shoes and leapt up onto the bed. He bounced tentatively to check if the ceiling was high enough for him to jump up and down without hitting his head. Then he started bouncing around crazily.

"Stop! Stop!" Blair shrieked. She stood up and took

Nate's hands, and they bounced together like a couple of demented, overgrown kids.

Then Nate stopped bouncing, suddenly serious. "So, um, does this mean something?"

Blair held on to his hands, swinging them from side to side. "Mean something?" she asked. "As in, are we back together?"

Nate shrugged his shoulders. "Yeah."

Blair blushed again, more deeply this time. "Well, we better be, because I love you too." Nate grinned and took a bouncy step forward so that his chin brushed her forehead. Blair tipped her head back. His gold-flecked green eyes sparkled. And then he kissed her.

It wasn't like they had a lot more to say.

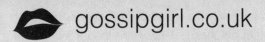

Disclaimer: All the real names of places, people, and events have been altered or abbreviated to protect the innocent. Namely, me.

hey people!

Isn't fate funny? You think you've got some control over things, you think you're in charge of life, but really, come on—we're all just at the mercy of the universe. I mean, we all read our horoscopes, don't we? And we all know there are some people who are just . . . connected. It doesn't always make sense, but it's not worth fighting. So I'm happy to report an early-bird sighting: **B** slipping out of the van der Woodsens' master bedroom to grab a fresh bottle of water, wearing **N**'s olive green polo (and nothing else). It's just fate, people. Get used to it.

The postparty e-mails are starting to trickle in, and it seems the big blowout was every bit as eventful as a Costume Institute gala. Minus the gowns—or any clothes whatsoever. But the thing everyone's talking about is the birthday girl and the boy who must've been her present . . . So, my faithful readers, I've got a poll for you:

You bump into an old flame. What do you do?

a) Adopt a vaguely Russian accent and go straight for the vodka.

b) Make out with the nearest quasi-cutie—nothing like a new flame to make him jealous.

c) Reminisce about old times . . . and then show him all your new tricks.

d) Call **S** and ask for advice—she's been there, done all of the above!

That's right: It seems that not only did **N** and **B** do some reuniting, but **S** got reacquainted with an old friend, **H**. Or more than a friend? He was seen carrying her into her bedroom just before daybreak. Awww. How sweet! Now give me the dirt. Who is he and what's the story? I'm dying for answers, and I know you are too!

your e-mail

Dear GG,
Just a response to your APB: I totally just spotted a vintage roadster while I was out for my morning run. It was parked in a long white gravel driveway and it looked like there were people sleeping in it together! Ew!
—5K

Dear 5K,
Congrats on sticking to your morning regimen, and thanks for the hot tip. But as usual, I'm way ahead of the game. The errant threesome has been located and I'm all boned up on what's going on. Let's just hope your sleeping beauties wake up before they return!
—GG

a little friendly advice

As city dwellers, we're used to waking up in our own beds. You can party anywhere, all night long, and a taxi is just waiting to whisk you back to your penthouse or town house. But it's different in the country. Everyone just . . . *sleeps over.* I know, I know. It sounds a little gross—waking up in some unfamiliar house, very likely with some unfamiliar hookup drooling on your skirt. And yes, it can be awkward seeing everyone in the unforgiving light, without the benefit of booze-goggles. But I'm in the giving mood, (hello, when am I not?), and I've got some advice . . .

five morning-after pointers

1) Country houses have the nicest bathrooms. Take a nice steam and feel free to bring a friend. The shower's big enough for two, and sharing is caring!

2) Yes, you look like a mess. So feel free to go ahead and borrow something from the host. But if you take some undies, just keep 'em. It'll be our secret.

3) Head hurts? Gather up the leftover champagne for mimosas, and slip a little Kahlúa into the cafetière. It might just get the party restarted.

4) Help yourself to the lady of the house's beauty products. Mommies always have the very best eye cream.

5) Still not feeling any better? There may still be some prescription-strength Motrin leftover from Granny's fall. Hey, hangovers *hurt*!

Okay, kids, time for me to take my own advice and follow it up with a little dip in the pool. Which pool? Oh, wouldn't you like to know?

You know you love me.

gossip girl

birthday blues

"Happy birthday to me," Serena whispered, her voice hoarse and scratchy. She slipped out of her rumpled canopy bed and yawned miserably. She'd been miserably half-asleep and half-awake all night, unable to doze off soundly with Henry cuddled up next to her. Nate's words kept repeating in her head: *I love you, I love you, I love you.*

Sliding her feet into her hot pink rubber flip-flops, she thwacked out of the bedroom. There was no need to tiptoe— Henry was snoring heavily enough that she could probably do an aerobics routine on the bed without disturbing him.

The hallway was quiet, and pale early morning sun peeked in through the massive windows. She lingered by the glass momentarily, taking in the view: the green expanse of the wide lawn, the calm glimmer of the swimming pool, the clear blue sky without even a suggestion of a cloud overhead. It was going to be another gorgeous day, but somehow the beautiful weather just made her feel more miserable.

Who knew she had a secret dramatic streak?

Hugging her bare arms, Serena descended the grand

main staircase down to the marble-tiled foyer, surveying the party damage: glass tumblers with the sticky remnants of mostly finished cocktails lining the entryway console table, stubbed-out cigarette butts strewn on the floor, abandoned paper plates filled with half-eaten hamburgers strewn absent-mindedly on the coffee table. Heading into the living room, she glanced around at the sleeping partygoers lolling listlessly on the tufted leather sofas, empty liquor bottles lying defeated at their sides.

Hope the maid's coming in today!

She studied the faces of the sleeping revelers—dozing and peaceful, not yet mindful of the horrid hangovers that were their immediate future. Everyone looked so sweet and innocent. Only a few hours before, they'd all joined in a rousing drunken chorus of "Happy Birthday." She'd pretended not to notice how they mumbled when they got to the "dear Serena" part. Besides Erik and Henry, the only other people at the party who knew her name were too busy upstairs to sing.

She found a clean tumbler in the kitchen and filled it with cold water, sipping it greedily to wash the taste of morning breath from her tongue.

Yum.

Hopping up on the counter, she perched for a while, feeling like the last person alive after a nuclear bomb or some other disaster. But the quiet helped her clear her mind. Today was her eighteenth birthday, but she wasn't thinking about what was ahead. For the first time in a long, long time, she couldn't stop thinking about the past.

Everyone always assumed that she was as happy-go-lucky

as she acted, but the truth was, she *was* acting. At least, some of the time. After all, even she looked liked crap when she'd been crying. And during those early days at Hanover she'd cried a *lot*.

She hopped off the counter and padded back into the library, sliding open the many small drawers of her father's heavy wooden desk until she unearthed some stationery. Then, instead of taking a seat in his giant leather office chair, she tucked herself under the desk. It had been one of her favorite hiding places when she was little. Dark and cozy and safe, with the dank scent of antique wood. She tucked the swivel chair in so she was completely hidden and started to write. By the time she'd said what she needed to, she'd filled three pages of the ivory-colored Crane's writing paper.

Climbing out of her hiding place, Serena stuffed the pages into an envelope and sealed it with two quick licks. She scrawled a name across the front of it, and then, moving quickly so she wouldn't lose momentum or second-guess herself, she hurried out of the house and into the driveway. Dozens of cars were parked half on and half off the lawn, but it was easy to spot the vintage hunter green Aston Martin, top still down, dewy and shining in the gray-gold morning light. She strode toward it purposefully, popped open the glove compartment, and left the envelope inside, faceup.

Somebody's in for a big surprise.

Air Mail - Par Avion - July 14

Dear Dan,

Wow—that's some big news! Maybe we can go shopping together when I get back? Or ice-skating? Do you like stuff like that now?

I was talking to Mom about it and she said that when you were little you were always hiding in her closet, trying on her sequined dresses from the seventies. Isn't that funny? Congratulations on finally coming out of the closet!

I love you!

Jenny

my baby takes the morning train

"I'm home," Vanessa whispered as she quietly shuffled into Dan's sprawling Upper West Side apartment. She carefully deposited her backpack on an armchair laden with winter coats even though it was July. It was only eight o'clock in the morning and it didn't seem fair to wake the whole household just to announce her definitely untriumphant return. How many times would she slink back here? It was basically the only place she had in the world to call home, and already she'd had to retreat there a distressing number of times in the past few weeks: first, after being unceremoniously evicted from the Williamsburg apartment, then after being fired from her first real job working on *Breakfast at Fred's,* and now after narrowly escaping a stint as a careless nanny and then vapid muse to the maniacally enthusiastic Bailey Winter.

Some summer!

"Who's there?"

Slightly startled to hear Dan's voice—at least it *sounded* like Dan—so early in the morning, Vanessa squinted into the still-dark hallway. "Dan? It's me. Vanessa."

"Vanessa," Dan muttered sadly. He was paler than usual, and his cheeks had a dusting of irregular stubble over them, like he'd started to shave and then changed his mind. Eggplant-colored circles ringed his eyes, and he was clutching an unlit cigarette in his hand as if he'd forgotten to light it and then forgotten it was there.

Wow—someone really isn't a morning person.

"Dan? You look like—" She paused, taking in the oily sheen of his unwashed, matted hair. She was suddenly overwhelmed with the feeling of wanting to draw him a bath and make him some oatmeal. She vaulted forward, sweeping him up in her arms. He smelled like musty cigarettes and armpit, but for some reason Vanessa still found it comforting. But just as she leaned in a little closer, smelling his spottily shaven neck, he stepped out of her embrace. "Are you okay?" she demanded, concerned.

"I don't know." Dan stuck the unlit cigarette into the corner of his mouth and patted his pockets miserably. "I can't find my lighter." He sounded almost on the verge of tears.

"Your lighter?" It didn't sound like that was his only problem. Poor Dan, sometimes he took imitating Keats a little too much to heart.

"It doesn't matter." Dan removed the cigarette from his mouth and tucked it behind his ear, where a mass of his slick, dirty hair kept it in place. "I'm going to make some coffee. You want some?"

Really, all she wanted to do was collapse into bed, possibly with Dan, but he was acting entirely bizarre. Plus he smelled weird.

"Coffee sounds good." Vanessa placed her arm gently

around Dan's shoulders, as though he was a delicate waif in need of comforting. She led him down the brown-rice-colored hallway toward the kitchen. "Maybe *I'll* make it, and you can just sit and tell me why you're such a mess."

Dan shuffled down the hallway after her but hadn't even made it to the kitchen before the words exploded out of him. "I let this dude I met at the Strand kiss me. We started a salon together. I'm gay. My dad said he did some gay stuff when he was hanging out with poets back in the day, but me—I'm really gay."

Vanessa brushed past him and into the kitchen. She unscrewed the lid on the commercial-size jar of Folgers instant coffee on the counter. Dan sat down at the worn Formica table and sank his head in his hands.

"What do you mean you 'started a salon'?" she demanded, totally ignoring the gay part of the equation. "You're Mr. Never Get a Real Haircut. What do you know about salons?"

Dan had to smile. "No, a literary salon. A *sa*lon," he repeated with the correct intonation. He stopped smiling. God, he sounded gay. "There were lots of pretty girls at our first meeting, and they were kissing each other too." He frowned, totally confused. "But I kissed Greg."

Vanessa microwaved a pitcher of water and poured it out into two mismatched mugs, stirring in spoonfuls of instant coffee. She took a sip and made a face. Christ, Folgers fucking tasted like dog piss after all the amazing coffee she'd been drinking in the Hamptons.

"So let me get this straight." She took another sip of the acrid coffee and looked across the room, past the mountain of unwashed dishes and the bowl of decomposing bananas to the rickety stool where Dan was perched miserably. "No pun intended."

"Ha," Dan said joylessly.

"So . . . you're gay. You. Dan Humphrey. Gay. Not gay happy-gay. Gay-gay. Gay, I-like-to-kiss-boys gay." Vanessa raised her dark eyebrows doubtfully.

"I wouldn't exactly say I *like* to kiss boys." Dan frowned. "But I did."

Jesus. She'd only been gone three days and Dan had already met someone else. Girl, boy, monkey. It just seemed kind of fast. "Well, I ate a salad once. Doesn't mean I'm a vegetarian."

"It's not that simple. I got a postcard from Jenny that said my mom said I used to wear dresses when I was a kid." Dan ran his fingers through his hair, inadvertently destroying the cigarette he'd tucked behind his ear only a few minutes before. "Shit."

"It kind of *is* simple, Dan. Look, you're either gay or you're not. Or . . ." Vanessa paused, considering this third option. "You're bi. Maybe that's what it is. You're just . . . exploring. Discovering yourself."

"Do you think so?" Dan's face brightened momentarily. "I mean, Greg's nice. We like the same things. But last night, when he was here, it totally freaked me out. And I didn't kiss him again. I just couldn't."

Part of Vanessa still wanted to be annoyed Dan had been kissing someone else while she had been, *ew,* considering Chuck Bass as a substitute for Dan, but she couldn't help but be moved by his pathetic state of total confusion. The little furrow in his brow looked like it had been there for days, and the defeated slope of his shoulders made her want to carry him to his room and tuck him in like a baby. And then do it with him.

But she brushed that thought aside for a moment. Dan was gay, or maybe bi. But he'd also been a lot of other things at different times: a toast-of-the-town literary sensation, a one-night-only rock god, a rebellious senior graduation speaker, a fitness freak. Now he was gay. It couldn't possibly last longer than any of his other phases, and when he got tired of being gay or he realized that being gay would mean actually kissing guys and not girls—her in particular—well, she'd be in the bedroom right next door.

"Look, Dan." Vanessa poured the rest of her bitter coffee into the crowded sink and left her mug on the countertop. "You need to stop being so hard on yourself. I mean, there's nothing *wrong* with being gay, is there?"

"Of course not! Thomas Mann was gay. And he won the Nobel Prize."

"Right." Vanessa grinned, pleased to hear Dan sounding a little more like himself. So predictable, so easily influenced. Let him get this gay stuff out of his system; she could wait. "So . . . I'd love to meet this Greg guy."

"Yeah?" Dan responded skeptically. "Really?"

"Yeah." Vanessa squeezed his shoulder. Now that Dan was gay, she could do things like sit on his lap, right? She decided to try it. "Really," she added, perching on Dan's bony knee. Dan slipped his arms around her waist and buried his nose between her shoulder blades.

"Thanks," he said, his voice muffled. "You're my hero."

Hey, maybe he really *is* gay.

nice e-mail address, buddy . . .

TO: Song of Myself <undisclosed recipients>
FROM: Greg P. <wilde_and_out@rainbowmail.net>
Re: Song of Myself's Next Meeting!

Dear Friends,

I hope you enjoyed getting together as
much as I did. I'm happy to report that our
first get-together has already resulted in
some burgeoning romances—a happy consequence
of bringing together so many like-minded
creative individuals. I hope we can continue
to inspire and excite one another at all
our meetings!

For our next get-together, please bring
along your favorite work of Shakespeare
and we'll take turns reading aloud. You
show me yours and I'll show you mine!

Yours in love and iambic pentameter,
Greg

on the road again

"Pull over!"

"What?" The one disadvantage of his dad's convertible was that it made having a conversation while driving almost impossible. Nate turned to see Blair frantically pointing at a sign announcing one of those cheesy scenic viewpoints where a couple of minivans were already parked along the shoulder.

Bo-ring.

"You want me to stop?" Nate had already slowed and was pulling over. He knew better than to argue with Blair.

"It'll be funny." Blair dug into her hastily packed Coach straw carryall and unearthed a digital camera. "I swiped it from Serena's house. I hope she's not too pissed."

Nate frowned at the mention of Serena's name. He was still feeling a little guilty about sneaking out of Serena's place without saying goodbye—and on her birthday. Blair had persuaded him that Serena wouldn't have wanted a morning wake-up call, birthday or no birthday, and chances were she hadn't gone to bed alone anyway. And it was her house, so it wasn't like they'd just ditched her in the middle of nowhere.

Whatever you need to tell yourself.

Before Nate had even turned off the car, Blair had already slipped out of her seat and skipped toward the low stone wall that separated the parking area from the dramatic drop-off into a deep, tree-lined valley below. She was wearing the tiniest white shorts he had ever seen, and they made her legs look ridiculously touchable. She hopped up onto the wall and pouted her lips.

"Take a picture!"

Grinning and horny all over again, Nate fumbled with his seat belt and burst out of the car, willing himself not to run over to the stone wall and stick his hands down her tiny shorts. He took the camera from Blair's outstretched hand instead. "Say cheese."

Blair stuck out her tongue and crossed her eyes.

"Gorgeous." Nate laughed at tan, happy, beautiful Blair on the little LCD screen.

Blair patted the wall next to her. "Take one of both of us together."

Nate clambered up on the wall and held the camera out in front of them. Blair pressed her smooth cheek against his. The smell of her made him feel lightheaded, and he put his free hand out to steady himself.

Careful there, slugger.

"I want our whole summer to be just like this." Blair slipped her arm through his and sighed. "The two of us, alone on the open sea. No people, no worries. It'll be perfect." Just like in the movie set on constant replay in her mind.

Nate nodded. "I can't wait to get out on the water." The

mental image of Blair in her bikini, lolling about on the deck of the *Charlotte,* swept over him. It was happening at last. The real summer he was meant to have was beginning—and everything was falling into place. Driving northeast in the serene summer afternoon toward the ocean, toward freedom, with Blair right next to him . . . Nate could feel the weight of all his past mistakes lift off of his shoulders. He had never swiped from his coach's stash of Viagra; he had never had his diploma withheld; he had never hooked up with Tawny; he had never rubbed ointment on Babs's tattoo. He had just spent the night with Blair, and he was about to spend the rest of the summer with her and maybe the rest of his life. All was as it should be with the universe.

"Okay. Time to drive." It was almost like Blair was reading his mind. She hopped down from the wall, grabbing the camera from Nate's hand to scrutinize the pictures he'd just taken.

"I just gotta make a pit stop." He nodded in the direction of the concrete bungalow that housed the roadside restrooms.

"Be quick about it." Blair kissed his cheek before skipping back to the passenger seat.

Inside the chemical-smelling bathroom, Nate focused on what would happen a couple of hours from that moment, when they at last reached their destination. He closed his eyes, picturing Blair skipping ahead of him, up the gangplank and onto the yacht, shedding those tiny white shorts as she went.

As he washed his hands, Nate felt the familiar throb of his phone vibrating in the pocket of his cargo shorts. It was probably Blair, telling him to hurry up. He smiled. Some things never changed—like Blair's impatience. He dialed his voicemail, hoping to listen to the sexy message Blair had left him as he dried his hands. The phone was perched precariously between his ear and his shoulder and he almost dropped it into the sink when instead of hearing Blair's sly, giggly voice, he heard the angry grumble of Coach Michael's.

"Archibald, I don't know what the hell you think you're pulling, but you better be on your deathbed right now. Thought my wife would cover for you? Forget it, kid. She said you were smoking pot in my fucking attic. Under my goddamn roof. You think I was bluffing, Archibald? I'm calling your dad the second I get off the phone. It's over, kid. You're never going to see that diploma. Yale? It's never going to happen. Big mistake, kid, fucking with me. Big-time mistake. And I'm not through with you yet."

Nate finished drying his hands on his shorts, then grabbed the phone, stabbing at the button that would erase that message forever. He stuffed it back in his pocket and studied his face in the cracked rest-stop mirror. He had to get the fuck out of there.

Spoken like a man on the run.

the purloined letter

"Hey. It's Blair. I just wanted to call and say, you know, happy birthday. Sorry we took off. I'll call you later and tell you everything."

Snapping her telephone shut and tossing it into her bag, Blair leaned back into the warm leather embrace of her bucket seat and tapped her foot impatiently. What the fuck was taking so long? The sooner they got back on the road, the sooner they would be at the *Charlotte*, and the sooner she would be stretched out on the wide wooden deck sunning herself in only her undies, drinking spiked lemonade and feeding Nate slivers of raw bluepoint oysters with her fingers. That's how she planned to spend every minute of the rest of the summer.

Not a bad plan!

She swiveled the rearview mirror to examine her face: her eyes looked bright and clear, her skin sun-kissed and flawless, her hair flecked with gold. She grinned at herself. All the stresses of the summer just melted away: she'd never gone to London with Lord Marcus; she'd never played second fiddle to Serena on her movie debut; she'd never seen Nate holding hands with some tacky Long Island townie. Everything was just as it should be: her and Nate, in love, forever.

Blair fiddled idly with the stereo, but Nate had the car keys in his pocket, so it wouldn't play. Impatiently, she turned the knob on the glove box. It dropped open to reveal a crisp white envelope with a name scrawled across it in a familiar hand.

Nate.

"What's this?" Blair said aloud. She picked up the envelope. Why the fuck was Serena leaving an envelope for Nate? Glancing in the direction of the bathroom to confirm that Nate was still inside, she slid her fingernail under the envelope's flap. She unfolded the paper and started to read Serena's manic scribble:

Nate: I just turned eighteen a couple of hours ago. When the clock struck, I looked around the room and I couldn't find you. I know you were with Blair, and if you're really happy, then I'm happy for you. Because how can you not want someone you love to be happy? But that's the thing, Nate . . . I think I love you. I know that sounds crazy, and there were so many other times I should have told you, but it didn't hit me until last night or tonight or whatever, and if I didn't tell you now, when would I have? It's just—it's always been you. Did you ever wonder why I came back last fall? Last night, when—

Blair stopped reading midsentence, flipping impatiently through the packet, three pages of heavy writing paper completely covered with Serena's too-big looping script. Her heart pounded in her chest. There was no question what to do next. She looked left and right just to confirm that she was indeed alone, then slipped out of the car and walked back to the scenic viewpoint.

Carefully, she tore the first page of the letter in half, then tore that half into quarters, and kept shredding it until all that remained was a handful of confetti, which she cupped in her palm. The warm breeze lifted the scraps of paper out of her hand and sent them showering onto the valley below. She did the same with the two other pages and the envelope as well, tearing them into tiny bits so that Serena's handwriting was just a jumble of meaningless shapes that the wind lifted and sent drifting into the valley below.

Blair returned to the car and reached into her bag to retrieve her cell phone. She studied the phone momentarily. Should she call Serena? Tell her that she knew all about the letter, that she knew how her supposedly best fucking friend actually felt about her boyfriend? Or should she just play innocent, ignore that two-faced bitch and focus on the perfect summer that stretched out before her? She suddenly didn't feel quite so bad about ditching Serena on her birthday.

No kidding.

"Ready to go?" Nate slid into the driver's seat, a boyish grin stretching across his perfect face.

"Ready." Blair pulled on her seat belt.

Buckle up—you're in for a wild ride!

better late than never?

Serena was once again lying in her all-white bed staring at the ceiling, trying to sleep now that she'd finally admitted how she really felt. The ceiling was pockmarked where she'd peeled off dozens of glow-in-the-dark stars just before she left for Europe, and she'd been counting the remaining stars for the last three hours, ever since she'd slipped the note into the Aston Martin. She kept losing count and starting again. And maybe she'd dozed off, or maybe not. Henry shifted onto his side, throwing his arm across her chest. It felt heavy and suffocating. She'd already been in this exact place, exactly a year before: in love with Nate, but lying next to Henry. She'd even admitted it and gotten it off her chest, so why couldn't she sleep?

Second thoughts?

She slid out of bed for the second time that morning and slipped into the hallway. Downstairs a few people were clanking bottles into the trash and whispering about their headaches. From the grandfather clock downstairs she heard that it wasn't morning anymore at all: it was exactly noon. She yanked at the long white T-shirt she was wearing. It said BROWN in capital letters across her chest and hung below her knees.

She didn't even know where she was walking until she got there, but she soon found herself in front of her parents' closed bedroom door. She knew that Blair and Nate were inside. They'd probably made a fort out of the many oversize pillows on the bed, which Blair had dubbed the Kissing Cave or something cheesy . . . or totally adorable if you were in love. Which Nate was. With Blair.

So what was Serena doing declaring her love for him now? There were so many other, better times she could have told him in the last year. Like when they were nearly naked in a Bergdorf's dressing room. Or when they were kissing in the bathtub at Isabel Coates's Hamptons house. Or when she'd decided not to go back to boarding school and came back to the city instead. But she hadn't. She hadn't told him any of those times, mostly because she'd been scared. That he didn't love her back, which he didn't. He loved Blair.

She backed away from the heavy wooden door that led to her parents' master bedroom suite and toward the stairs where Nate had told Blair he loved her just last night. So why had she suddenly declared *her* love for Nate, now, at the very worst possible time?

"Hey, you're the birthday girl." A guy she'd never seen before looked up at her from the bottom of the staircase. His shaggy brown hair was piled on top of his head in a messy bun. "Selima, right?"

"Serena," she told him.

"Right, so like, do you think you can give me a ride to the

train station?" He reached under his sweat-stained and moth-eaten polo to scratch his belly, revealing a sliver of hairy stomach.

Ew.

Serena took a step down the stairs, letting her hand glide over the dark wooden banister. "I'm sure people will start getting up soon. Someone will drive you."

"Cool." He stretched his arms up high, yawning loudly, and headed back into the living room, where people were still sprawled out on every soft surface. She heard someone mutter "*Duuuuude,*" as he collapsed onto the antique buttoned-leather couch.

Serena swept through the marble foyer to the door and lingered for a moment, hand on the doorknob, before she pulled the door open and stepped outside. The front of the house was well shaded and cool, and she wrapped her arms around her body protectively as she scanned the driveway.

She wasn't sure if she was having second thoughts, or not, or if she wanted to sneak back to that car and take back the envelope she'd left inside. But the decision had been made for her. The Aston Martin was nowhere in sight. Nate— and presumably Blair—were gone.

And they'd taken some very juicy reading material along with them.

sailing off into the sunset

Blair knelt in the bucket seat of the car as Nate slowed the Aston Martin to a stop in front of the whitewashed Newport Yacht Club. The harbor glimmered in the midday sun. Blair breathed in the warm, salty seaside air. She kept shaking her head, letting her windblown locks swing around her shoulders, which she hoped looked sexy. In truth, she was just trying to shake the thought of Serena's letter from her mind. Seriously, what the fuck?

"I can't believe we're actually here." Nate's voice startled her back to attention. Despite having driven for hundreds of miles just to get there, Nate didn't seem all that eager to get out of the car. He'd undone his seat belt and was just sitting there, staring out of the car's tiny windshield at the forest of masts in the harbor.

"What's wrong?" Blair opened the door and hopped up and down, getting the blood in her legs flowing again.

"What? Oh, nothing." Nate looked startled.

Blair settled her fists on her hips. Her blousy cotton voile shirt fluttered in the wind. "Are you sure everything's okay? You look kind of . . . distracted."

"No, no, everything's fine." Nate stood and slammed his door shut behind him. "We'll have to do something about the car, I guess." He frowned.

Blair adjusted her bag and perched on the still-warm hood of the hunter-green Aston. Nate looked more than distracted. He looked like he was going to throw up. Was there any chance he knew about the letter? Or could Serena have called him while he was in the restroom? Was that why he'd taken so long? Blair fidgeted impatiently. What was the holdup? "Nate, is there anything you want to tell me?"

"What? No," Nate answered, stuffing the keys in his pocket. "We're really doing this, right?"

"We're really doing this!" Leaving her bag on the hood of the car, Blair scurried around to where Nate stood and threw herself into his arms. A white seagull swooped down onto the parking lot. "You seem worried."

"No, I'm not. I'm just . . . thinking is all."

Don't hurt yourself.

Inhaling Nate's delicious scent—his deodorant, a hint of the lavender soap from Serena's parents' master bathroom, the ocean smell that had somehow already made it into his shirt—Blair closed her eyes. "Don't worry, Natie. It's summer. And we're together. That's all that matters, isn't it?"

Nate pulled away just far enough to look at her face. She smiled up at him, hoping for a moment that they'd get shipwrecked somewhere and that they'd never have to see Serena again. They'd live in a bamboo hut, forage for food, and be naked all the time. Who needed clothes when they had each other?

She must be out of her mind.

"You're right. Fuck it. Fuck everything and everyone else." Then he bent down and pressed his delicious mouth to hers. "Let's get out of here."

Be sure to send a postcard.

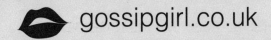 gossipgirl.co.uk

Disclaimer: All the real names of places, people, and events have been altered or abbreviated to protect the innocent. Namely, me.

hey people!

You know what's totally lame? Happy endings. Seriously. Like when I'm at the movies and see some plucky, determined girl finally land her leading man—whom I knew for the past two hours she'd end up with anyway—I just want to claw her eyes out. Real life is actually terribly messy and complicated and nothing ever just *ends* . . . I mean really, if you'll allow me get all philosophical about it for a minute, every ending is really just another beginning, isn't it? Okay, I'll shut up now.

So while **B** and **N** may be sailing off into the sunset, something tells me this story is far from over. Especially when there are so many questions waiting to be answered. Like:

Will **B** tell **N** about the letter from **S**?

Will **S** find **N** and tell him on her own?

Will **B** throw her overboard if she does?

Will **D** really make out with another boy? Again. Will they go even further?!

Will **V** really cheer him on if he does?

And realistically how long can those two stay roommates and not bedmates? Maybe he's bi after all.

Then of course there's the biggest question of all: Who am *I*? I know you guys are totally craving for more dirt on me, so here's an interesting tidbit about yours truly (Don't say I never give you anything!): I just can't keep a secret. I mean, except for the secret of who I am, of course. But secrets like the one **S** has been keeping all these years? Hats off to her! I can understand fooling your friends and even your family, but if you can manage to keep me in the dark, well, bravo! So what else is she hiding? I have a feeling there's a lot more to be discovered here . . .

I know you're dying for answers. Well, me too. And you know I always get what I want.

You know you love me.

gossip girl

Read the other fantastically GOSSIPLICIOUS titles
in the Gossip Girl series …